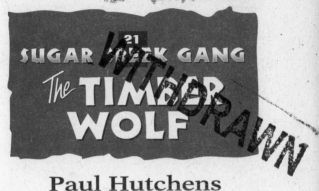

SUGAR CREEK GANG
The TIMBER WOLF

Paul Hutchens

MOODY PRESS
CHICAGO

© 1957, 1998 by
PAULINE HUTCHENS WILSON

Revised Edition, 1998

All Scripture quotations are taken from the *New American
Standard Bible,* © 1960, 1962, 1963, 1968, 1971, 1972,
1973, 1975, 1977, and 1994 by The Lockman Foundation,
La Habra, Calif. Used by permission.

Original Title: *Sugar Creek Gang at Snow Goose Lodge*

ISBN: 0-8024-7025-4

5 7 9 10 8 6 4

Printed in the United States of America

PREFACE

Hi—from a member of the Sugar Creek Gang!

It's just that I don't know which one I am. When I was good, I was Little Jim. When I did bad things—well, sometimes I was Bill Collins or even mischievous Poetry.

You see, I am the daughter of Paul Hutchens, and I spent many an hour listening to him read his manuscript as far as he had written it that particular day. I went along to the north woods of Minnesota, to Colorado, and to the various other places he would go to find something different for the Gang to do.

Now the years have passed—more than fifty, actually. My father is in heaven, but the Gang goes on. All thirty-six books are still in print and now are being updated for today's readers with input from my five children, who also span the decades from the '50s to the '70s.

The real Sugar Creek is in Indiana, and my father and his six brothers were the original Gang. But the idea of the books and their ministry were and are the Lord's. It is He who keeps the Gang going.

PAULINE HUTCHENS WILSON

1

Our six sets of Sugar Creek parents expected us to have a very safe and sane winter vacation at the Snow Goose Lodge.

They expected it because our camp director was to be Barry Boyland, Old Man Paddler's nephew. Barry had taken us on two north woods summertime trips, and we'd not only come back alive but were, as they expressed it, "better boys than when we went."

We had gone South once in the winter, all the way down to the Mexican border. We'd gone up North twice in the summer, but never before had we spent a week in the north woods in the winter. Our folks seemed to think it would be good for us to have the experience of ice fishing, skiing, playing boys' games around an open fire in a fireplace, and learning a little more about woodcraft and other things it is worthwhile for a boy to know and do.

It's a good thing our parents didn't know in advance that a one-hundred-pound timber wolf would be hanging around the lodge most of the time we were there.

And my mother's grayish-brown hair would have turned completely gray overnight if she had known that the weather in the Paul Bunyan Playground was going to be so unseasonably warm that it would wake up the hibernating bears—and that we would have an adventure with an honest-to-goodness live bear before our wonderful week was over.

Our folks certainly didn't imagine that after nearly a week of unseasonably warm weather, while the bears were still out, not having found their new winter quarters, a wild blizzard would come sweeping in and we would be caught out in it a long way from the lodge, not able to tell directions or to find our way back.

It's a very good thing our parents didn't know.

Of course, none of the gang knew it either. All we knew was that somewhere in the wilds of the North, near a town called Squaw Lake, on the shore of a lake by the same name, there was a lodge called the Snow Goose, and we were going to have a one-week winter vacation there.

The Snow Goose Lodge, as you maybe already know, if you've read the story named *The Green Tent Mystery*, was owned by the Everards, people who spent part of one wonderful summer camping in a green tent in our own Sugar Creek territory.

What you don't know, and maybe ought to before you get to the most exciting part of this story, is that our camp director, Barry Boyland, was studying in a Minneapolis college, and the vacation was for his education as well as ours.

"He's writing an important paper on 'Wildlife in the Frozen North,'" Mom said at the supper table one evening before we went.

"And you boys are to help him while you're there," Dad said across the table from me.

Mom's kind of bright remark in answer was: "You are not to *be* the wildlife, understand, but only to help Barry learn all he can about it."

I knew from what they had said, and the way they said it, that I was expected to behave myself even better than usual.

What else you don't know—and maybe would like to—is that this year the Everards had gone to California for the winter. The Gang and Barry would be alone at Snow Goose, except for the time Ed Wimbish, an old trapper, would spend with us.

The day finally arrived for us to leave. After we'd said our last good-byes to our envious fathers and our half-worried mothers, we were on the big bus and gone. Barry would meet us at Minneapolis. Then we'd spend the night in a hotel to get acquainted with what it is like to stay in a big city hotel. We'd start early the next morning in Barry's station wagon for the Snow Goose.

After we had traveled maybe twenty-five miles on the bus, Big Jim, who was sitting in the seat beside me, drew a letter from an inside pocket and said, "I got this just before we left. It's from the Everards."

I read the letter and felt my spine tingling with the kind of feeling I always get when I'm beginning to be scared. When I'd finished it, I passed it back, saying, "Better not let Little Jim and Dragonfly know about it. They're too little. They'd be s–scared."

There was no use keeping the secret from any of the other members of the gang, though. We'd all have to know sooner or later. So Big Jim let everybody read the letter, the scary part of which was:

> You won't need to be afraid of any of the wild-life you will see around the lodge. The bears are in hibernation, and the wolves are cowards and afraid of human beings. You'll probably not see even one wolf, unless it is Old Timber, which Mr. Wimbish will tell you about. We've never seen him ourselves. Ed calls him the ghost wolf because he always fades from sight a second after you see him—or so Ed says. But Ed exaggerates, and you can take some of what he says with several grains of salt.

"Sounds fishy to me," I said to Big Jim. I'd read stories about wolves, and in the stories they hadn't been afraid of human beings at all.

Poetry, who had brought his camera along, said, "I've always wanted a picture of a human ghost but could never get one. I'm going to try a ghost *wolf!*"

His tone of voice was light, but I knew from the way he looked at me that he was only talking that way to help keep Little Jim and Dragonfly from worrying.

When we got to Minneapolis, Barry met us and took us to the Hastings Hotel, where we had two big double rooms with a bath between them and an extra cot in each room.

Dragonfly tried to make us laugh by trying a very old and very worn-out joke on us. He said, "How come we have to have a bathtub when we aren't going to stay till Saturday night?"

"Quiet!" Big Jim ordered. "I'm phoning Sugar Creek to tell them we're all here and all right."

Dragonfly tried another joke, saying, "But some of us are not all *there*," which wasn't funny, either.

Soon Big Jim had his mother on the phone.

I was standing close by, looking out the window at a small snow-covered park with trees and shrubs scattered through it. My mind's eye was imagining Old Timber standing tall and savage-looking with his long tongue out, panting and looking up at us. Even though my thoughts were at Snow Goose Lodge, it was easy to hear what Big Jim was telling his mother and also to hear what her excited mother voice was saying to him. She could hardly believe we were there so soon.

Then all of a sudden there were what sounded like a dozen other mother voices on the party line, trying to give Big Jim special orders for their sons. Big Jim had a pencil in his hand and was grinning and writing. Then, all of a sudden he was holding out the phone to me, saying, "It's your mother. She wants to talk to you."

"Your compass, Bill," Mom said. "You left it

on the upstairs bureau. Be careful not to get lost in the woods. Better buy a new one if none of the other boys have any. You know you got lost up there once before—and also on Palm Tree Island."

It was good advice, although it worried me to have her worry about me.

"Don't worry," I said into the phone and maybe into the ears of five other mothers. "The sun shines up here too—the very same sun that shines down there—and we can tell directions by it anytime."

"Then be sure your watch is running and the time is right *all* the time," she ordered me. And I knew *she* knew the secret of telling directions on a sunshiny day if you had a watch and knew how to use a certain Scout trick. Mom was right, though. The watch had to be set correctly.

I guess a boy ought to be glad he has a mother to give him good advice, even if sometimes he doesn't need it because he already knows exactly what she is telling him.

While we were all getting our hair combed, our ties straight, our shoes touched up a little, and our coat collars brushed for dinner in the hotel, we tossed what we hoped were bright remarks at one another. Nobody got angry at anybody since it is a waste of good temper to lose it on a friend.

Nothing happened of any importance till after dinner, which at Sugar Creek we would have called supper.

I'd thought Barry seemed a little anxious

about something while we were in the dining room. He hardly noticed the pretty murals, except to tell us they were enlarged photographs in full color of actual cherry trees, with grass and dandelions underneath and a gravel road running past. They covered one whole wall of the dining room.

He kept looking around, and whenever what is called a "page" went through, calling out names of people wanted on the phone, he seemed to hope his own name would be called.

We hadn't any sooner gotten back to our rooms and settled down a little than the phone rang. I was closest to it and, in a mischievous mood, pretended a dignified voice and answered, saying, "Room 423, the Hastings Hotel. William Collins speaking."

I certainly felt foolish a second later when a woman's voice said, "May I speak to Barry, please—Mr. Boyland, I mean?"

I felt and heard myself gulp, then I answered, "Certainly. Just a moment."

I didn't have to call Barry, though. He had been sitting under a floor lamp on the other side of the room, reading a book called *Hunting in the Great Northwest* and taking notes with his green pen, maybe jotting down things he could quote in the important paper he was going to write for his college class.

Well, the very second the phone rang, he was out of his chair like a rabbit scared out of its hole. Almost before I could hand him the phone, he had it and was saying, "Hello!" in a voice that sounded as if he was all alone with somebody he liked extrawell and was telling her something nobody else was supposed to hear.

Maybe it wasn't polite for me to listen, but how could I help it? It wouldn't have been polite for me to stop my ears, would it?

I couldn't tell what the woman's musical voice on the other end of the line was saying, but Barry's deep-voiced answers were like a boy's hand stroking a baby rabbit in the palm of his other hand. He was talking to her about his trip into the frozen North and asking her not to worry, that he'd be all right.

"Yes," Barry was saying to the person I imagined was his age and was pretty and could smile like our Sugar Creek teacher, Miss Lilly. "I'll be careful. I have six bodyguards, you know."

And then, all of a sudden, Barry was saying, "Yes. I think I can run over for a few minutes."

He put down the phone, turned back into the room, and said, with excitement in his eyes but with a very calm voice, "I'll have to be gone for an hour or so, boys. You can wait here, or you may go down to the basement game room for Ping-Pong—but mind you, no disturbance! Remember who you are."

"Your mother worried about you, too?" Little Jim asked, and I knew he was thinking that whoever called Barry was Barry's own mother, giving him last-minute instructions to take care of himself.

Barry looked at Little Jim with a faraway

expression in his eyes. Then he grinned and answered, "Every good mother worries a little."

Maybe I shouldn't have said what I did just then, but I might not have been able to help it even if I'd tried. This is what came out of my mind as I answered Little Jim, "His mother is maybe only about twenty years old."

Barry shot me a quick look with a grin in it and right away put in a phone call for a taxi. He got his heavy brown storm coat out of the closet, put it on, brushed a few flecks of dust off its dark-brown mouton collar, took another look in the mirror at his hair, ran his hand over his chin to see if he needed a shave, decided he didn't—or if he did, he wouldn't have time to give himself one—and a minute later was out the door and gone.

His idea that we might want to go to the game room in the basement was a good one. So pretty soon, Big Jim, who had charge of us, gave the order, and pretty soon after that we were in the basement playing noisy sets of the same kind of table tennis we sometimes played in Poetry's basement back home.

I watched for my chance to talk to Poetry alone for a few minutes, because I had something special on my mind. When he and I finished a game and handed our paddles to Dragonfly and Little Jim, we took the elevator to the hotel lobby.

We knew it wasn't supposed to be good for a boy to eat hard-to-digest candy before going to bed, so we bought the kind of candy bar we liked best and hoped it wouldn't be hard to digest.

Poetry said, as he unwrapped his, "My jaw muscles haven't had any exercise since we were eating dinner beside the cherry trees."

"Supper," I said.

"Dinner," he countered and added, "the people back at Sugar Creek are behind the times!"

We were in two big leather-upholstered chairs behind a potted palm at the time. Ignoring what Poetry thought was a bright remark, I told him about the cheerful woman's voice I'd heard on the phone, asking for Barry. "She wasn't any more his mother than the man in the moon is a man," I said.

Poetry let out a low whistle, squinted his eyes, then said, "Poor Barry," and shook his head sadly.

"How come you say *that*?" I asked.

He sighed, took another bite of his bar, shook his head again sadly, and answered, "Life is more fun being a boy—without growing up and having a girl to worry about."

Neither of us said anything for a few minutes, while I thought about the happiness I'd seen in Barry's eyes when he was flying around the room getting his tie straight, his coat on, the dust off its lapels, and running his hand over his chin the way Dad does to see if he needs a shave.

There was a radio on in the hotel lobby, and somebody's voice was racing along very fast, giving a news program. My mind was so busy thinking about Barry and wondering where he was and when he would be back that I hardly noticed the news announcement about the weather. It was something about "unseasonably warm weather in northern Minnesota continuing for another week." I could see, out the hotel's large picture window, the stars twinkling in an absolutely clear sky.

Poetry and I, behind our potted palm— pretending we were in a climate where palm trees grow naturally, such as at the very bottom of the United States where we had spent a whole week's winter vacation with Mom and Dad and Dragonfly's parents—sat munching away, talking dreamily about imaginary things:

"See those seagulls up there, tossing around in the hot summer air?" he asked.

I answered lazily, "Don't make me open my eyes. I'm too sleepy here on this sandy beach under this palm tree."

"All right, then. See those snow geese flying? See that beautiful white snow goose, with black wing tips and a pink beak, headed north to the lodge?"

I yawned lazily, my nine-o'clock-at-night imagination making me feel sleepy. "I don't know what Barry went after in such a hurry, but I wish he'd come back. It's my bedtime."

And that's when Barry came breezing into the lobby, and with him was a sparkling-eyed, rosy-cheeked girl in a dark green coat with wide fur sleeves and a fur collar. She was only about five-and-a-half feet tall and was laughing, as also was Barry. They didn't seem to know there was anybody in the world except each other. He was carrying a four-foot-long gun case with a luggage-type handle.

I looked at Poetry in his chair, and the two of us stayed as low as we could under the fronds of the potted palm.

Barry set down the gun case, and the two of them went outside again into the cold night.

In a flash, Poetry and I were out of our tropical climate to see what was going on outside, if anything.

What we saw wasn't any of our business, but since it happened right in front of our astonished eyes, we almost had to see it.

"What do you know about that?" Poetry exclaimed in a disappointed voice. "Poor Barry!" —the same thing he had said when we were still up in our room.

For about a minute Barry and the girl stood at the door of a taxi, whose driver was waiting for her to get in. Then, all of a sudden, they gave each other a half-long kiss, as I'd accidentally seen Mom and Dad give each other quite a few times back home. Barry helped her into the cab then, closed the door, and stood watching while the driver steered out into the night traffic and was gone.

By the time Barry was back inside, Poetry and I were walking around the lobby, looking with let's-pretend indifference at the pictures on the walls and at the many different kinds of candy bars at the hotel magazine stand.

Barry's voice behind us was certainly cheerful as he said, "You boys want a candy bar? Pick out your favorite. The treat's on me."

"No, thank you," Poetry said politely. "Candy at bedtime isn't good for a boy my size."

Just then, from the stairway leading to the basement game room came the rest of the gang, and there wasn't a one of *them* who thought a candy bar would be hard to digest before going to bed.

A little later we were all up the elevator and into our rooms, where Barry asked us, "Want to see what I went after?" He opened the gun case and took out one of the prettiest rifles I ever saw.

All our eyes lit up, Big Jim's and Circus's especially. "We may have to bring down a wolf, or maybe we can get a deer or two," Barry explained.

"Or a bear," Little Jim said with a grin, maybe remembering that he himself had once killed a fierce old mother bear back at Sugar Creek.

"This is what the phone call was about," Barry explained, looking at me out of the corner of his eye, which made me look around out of the corner of my eye at the other members of the gang. He was probably remembering I had said quite a while ago, after I'd heard the lady's musical voice on the phone—"His mother is maybe only twenty years old."

For a few seconds you could have heard a pine needle fall, everything was so extraquiet.

"You see," Barry added, "one of my classmates at college lives at Squaw Lake. She's a grandniece of Mr. and Mrs. Wimbish. When her own mother and father died, they sort of adopted her. This gun was her Christmas present to me. She had to order it from the East, so it was a little late getting here. Isn't it a beauty?"

I thought, as Barry talked, that it was indeed the prettiest repeater rifle I ever saw, with its crowned muzzle and raised-ramp front sight and gleaming walnut stock. Just looking at it made me tingle with anticipation at what an exciting and maybe even dangerous time we were going to have on our vacation.

My mind flew on ahead to the Snow Goose, so that I missed part of what Barry was telling us. I didn't come to until I heard him saying, ". . . so that's the way it is. Next June, just as soon as school is out up here, there'll be a wedding at the Snow Goose. You boys'll get to know her yourselves when she comes up the last of the week to bring the station wagon."

"The station wagon?" I exclaimed. "I thought *we* were going to ride up in it ourselves. I thought—"

"We *were* to have," Barry explained and started to untie his tie, getting ready to get ready for bed. "But I had to have the engine overhauled, and the mechanic ran into some serious trouble.

"Jeanne is letting us drive *her* car. Two of you," he added, as he slipped out of his shirt and I saw his powerful muscles like a nest of snakes under his tan skin, "two of you will have to ride the bus. There wouldn't be room in the car for all of us, along with all this luggage." He gestured around the room at our six different kinds of suitcases.

There was some friendly excitement for a while, as different ones of us begged Barry to let us ride the bus to Squaw Lake.

"It'll have to be two of the biggest ones of you," Barry decided.

"Biggest *tall* or biggest *around?*" Poetry asked hopefully.

That sort of settled it. Barry decided on Poetry for sure, and a little later, maybe because Poetry and I were such good friends, he picked me for the other one of the two.

Early in the morning we were off—Poetry and I on the bus, and the rest of the gang with Barry as soon as they could get the car serviced. As we pulled out of the gas station and headed out through the snowplowed streets toward the open country and the wild, frozen North, I was wondering how much sooner we would get to Squaw Lake than they would.

Poetry was wondering the same thing and said so. But he wasn't worried the least bit about what we would do to pass the time while we waited for them. Something else was on his mind. "Poor Barry! He's one of the finest woodsmen I know. He likes the out-of-doors, and nature studies, and camping out. What'll he do, marrying a citified girl like that—you know—like that extrapretty, helpless-looking girl we saw back there in the hotel?"

I sighed and looked out the window at the cars and trucks we were threading our way through, then back at Poetry's face. "Yeah, poor Barry! Poor Sugar Creek Gang too! We'll lose our camp director!"

Neither of us said anything for a while. For a minute I felt pretty sad, but Poetry cheered me up by saying, "But both our fathers got married once, and it didn't hurt them—not much, anyway."

Hearing that, my thoughts took a flying leap out across the sky to Sugar Creek, and I thought about what a fine person Theodore Collins was. Also I seemed to see him and Mom sitting at the breakfast table that very minute without me. They were pretty nice people. Both of them, I thought.

Answering Poetry, I said, "Yeah, but my father married a good farm girl, who knew how to work and could bake pies and cakes and do all the other things a farmer's wife has to do."

"My mother too," Poetry said proudly. Then he shook his head once more and added, "But I'm afraid Barry's got a girl who'll have to be waited on, and who won't want to camp out, and will be too dainty to rough it like he likes to do."

But we couldn't worry our heads about it. We had a long ride and a wonderful winter vacation ahead of us: ice fishing, running the trapline with Barry and Ed Wimbish, the old-timer trapper who, with his wife, Martha, once owned the Snow Goose but had sold it to the Everards.

Wildlife in the frozen North, that was what Barry was going up to study. How much wildlife would *we* see on our vacation? How *wild* would it be? And how *savage*? *Was* there an honest-to-goodness one-hundred-pound timber wolf hanging around the place, or was old Ed just an exaggerator as the Everards' letter had said?

We'd soon find out.

2

All the time our busload of people was roaring on into the North, I kept wondering how soon Barry's car had been serviced and whether, after they got started, they could drive fast enough to catch up with us—or if they'd have any trouble on the way.

Poetry asked me, as we ate a sandwich-and-milk lunch at a roadside cafe with all the other bus people, "What'll we do if the gang gets stuck in a drift and we have to spend the night —the first night—in the Snow Goose all by ourselves?"

Trying to be funny, I answered, "I don't know what *you'll* do, but I'll spend my night sleeping." My answer was smothered in a yawn. I certainly was drowsy, maybe from having had so little undisturbed sleep in the hotel last night.

I'd never been waked up so many times in one night in my whole life. First it had been Dragonfly, snoring like a saw cutting a rick of wood. Then it was Poetry, who was in the big double bed with me, rolling over in his sleep and threshing around with his arms and accidentally shoving me out onto the floor, where I landed with enough noise to wake up the rest of the gang and get several pillows thrown at me. Then it was the traffic outside in the street and all the lights of the cars parading across the ceiling.

Worst of all, though, it seemed there was something heavy in my stomach, as if maybe it hadn't been a good thing to eat that candy bar just before going to bed.

On the bus again and gone again, Poetry and I took a lazy nap apiece. In fact, we took several of them, making the time go faster.

The farther we went, the higher the snow-drifts were on either side of the highway, and it seemed there were millions of pine and spruce and fir and leafless trees everywhere, forests and forests and forests of them. The snow in the bright sunlight made it look as if we were driving on a long white-gold ribbon that wound round and round through a forest that didn't have any end. It was easy to imagine that the trees had big, white, very heavy blankets thrown over them.

I was dreaming out at the flying country-side, still half-sleepy, when Poetry spoke up and said, "Look! See that!"

"See *what?*" I asked, not interested in see-ing anything I had to open my eyes to look at.

"That lake!"

"What? *Where?*" That's all I had been seeing for hours, except for trees and more trees. Each lake looked like a Sugar Creek pasture covered with snow—not any water in sight and no ice either.

"Squaw Lake, I mean," Poetry yawned an answer to my yawned question.

I looked out the window and down the road through the bus's wide windshield, and there wasn't any sign of a lake.

"Here," Poetry explained, "on this map. It's only forty miles farther. We'll get there in less than an hour. The sun won't be down. We can go fishing and have fish ready for supper by the time the gang gets there."

The last forty miles were gone in only a little while, it seemed, and all of a sudden there was a screeching of bus brakes and a voice singing out, "Squaw Lake!"

We were off the bus, and it was gone in only a few minutes. Poetry and I were left standing in front of an oldish-looking store called "Wimbish Grocery." The weather was certainly mild, and it didn't feel nearly as cold as I thought it ought to be that far north.

"Hey!" Poetry exclaimed, with astonishment in his voice, looking all around at the same time. "Where's the town? Where's Squaw Lake?"

"Yeah! Where is it?" I asked, not seeing any.

"Oh, *there* it is!" he grunted. "Up there on the sign above the word 'Wimbish.'"

I looked and read, "Squaw Lake Post Office."

We looked at each other, wondering, *What on earth?*

"Where's the rest of the town?" I asked Poetry.

He looked all around, shading his eyes against the sun. "This is it. There isn't any rest of it."

And there wasn't, except for a few scattered houses, maybe six or seven, along what could have been Main Street if there had been one. Squaw Lake was only a grocery store that sold everything *inside* and gas *outside* at two red pumps.

As soon as we were inside, a heavyset lady with a smile as broad as her large, friendly face came waddling toward us, saying, "How do you do? What can I do for you?"

"We're part of the Sugar Creek Gang," Poetry's ducklike voice answered her ducklike waddle and her question.

"Well, I *am* glad to see you. The Everards told us all about you." She beamed at Poetry. "You just bring your luggage into the back. You may have to wait a spell. We've had a phone call from down the line, and the rest of your party is hung up with car trouble. You boys hungry?"

Before Poetry could say, "Certainly," as he always does in answer to a question like that, the phone rang somewhere in the store. The woman bustled her way down the narrow aisle between shelves of groceries and all kinds of stuff to the back of the store. Then I noticed the phone on the wall by a sign that read General Delivery.

I was worried about the rest of the gang. "What'll they do out on some country road in the cold with a broken-down car? What if they're miles and miles from a town?" I asked Poetry.

"Goose! *Snow* Goose!" he answered. "Where

do you think they telephoned from? A snow-drift?"

I sighed with relief, sorry I had been so dumb. "But what if they don't get here before night? Where'll *we* spend the night?"

"Snow Goose," he answered again.

While we'd been talking, the lady at the phone had been exclaiming and oh-ing and ah-ing, which was probably the same as saying, "What on earth?" She was also saying, "You don't say!" and "Oh, dear!" She would make a good Sugar Creek mother, I thought. I was wondering if the phone was a "party line" and how many Squaw Lake mothers were listening in.

Poetry brought my thoughts back to Squaw Lake by saying, "We'll have the time of our lives—just the two of us. We'll pretend we're hunters or explorers lost in the woods, and we'll accidentally happen onto an abandoned lodge in the forest and—"

He was interrupted by a little bell tinkling above the front door of the store. The door was whisked open, letting in a rush of cold air and a short, wiry, long-whiskered little old man. His movements were as nervous as a frisky dog's and as friendly as a puppy that comes wriggling all over the place up to you, wagging a friendly tail as much as to say, "Hi, everybody! I hope you like me as well as I like you."

The energetic little man didn't see us at first but took off his steamed-up glasses and called, "Marthy! Where are you? That sun's sure bright! Enough to blind a feller!"

From the telephone "Marthy" called back, saying, "Where've you been all afternoon?"

"Where've I *been*?" the little man said, cleaning his glasses with a tissue he had taken from a box on the counter. "I been out to the Snow Goose. I got the fire looked after and finished the road out to the fishing shanty. Seen anything of them Sugar Creek fellers?"

Marthy was still jabbering into the phone. I was hearing her say, "I never saw such weather for the middle of the winter—day after day after day of it. You never can tell. How's that? You don't say! Well, I swan."

Poetry beside me said, "*Not* swan! Snow Goose!"

The frisky little man had his glasses dry now and on again. He noticed Poetry and me for the first time and asked, "You the Sugar Creek boys that was a-coming up to stay at the Snow Goose?"

I felt a grin running up and down my spine, hearing the lively little man talk like that, because it was the way quite a few of the old-timers around Sugar Creek talked.

"I'm shore glad to see you young'uns," the bewhiskered, sawed-off, talkative man said, as soon as he found out we were two of the boys he'd been looking for.

Poetry grinned at me and I at him as he answered the little man in old-timer language. "The two of us young'uns came on the bus. The rest of the gang got hung up with car trouble down the road a piece and won't get here for quite a spell. I reckon we'd better get on out to the Snow Goose and get supper ready for them."

I knew Poetry wasn't joking when he talked about getting supper. He was the best cook of the whole gang and could even bake pies.

I certainly didn't expect the little man to take us up on the idea, though. I'd supposed that we'd have to stay at the Wimbish Grocery and Post Office and Service Station till Barry and the rest arrived, however long it might be, depending on whatever was wrong with the car.

But the frisky little man said he had a little more to do to get the Snow Goose ready. He was the caretaker for the Everards while they were gone. And Marthy didn't see anything against letting us go along for the ride, and "maybe they could do a mite of chores theirselves."

In a short while the little man was driving us out onto the snowplowed, pine-bordered highway and down it toward the place where pretty soon we'd see the first Snow Goose sign showing us where to turn to go to the lodge.

Riding beside the bewhiskered old man in the rattling Jeep, Poetry not only watched the scenery with me but was busy with pencil and paper, writing or drawing something. "Just in case we have to make the trip all by ourselves someday," he said, "I'm drawing a map."

Every time we came to a big Snow Goose sign, Poetry would quickly draw one on his map. The sign painter had certainly done a good job, I thought. Each sign had a large flying white goose having black-tipped wings and a reddish-pink beak pointing the way.

Finally we swung into a narrow lane wide enough for only one car at a time and winding through high drifts. After about a hundred yards the Jeep came to an abrupt halt, and our driver came to the quickest life a man his size ever came to. "Look, boys! There in the evergreens! That's *him!* That's Old Timber! The *ghost* wolf!"

I looked straight ahead to where Mr. Wimbish was pointing. First, I saw a little wooden house standing on four large, perpendicular, bark-covered logs. Then, at the foot of a narrow ladder leading up to the door, was what looked like the biggest police dog I ever saw.

"The ornery critter'd like to get his teeth into that quarter of venison I cached up there yesterday," Ed Wimbish exclaimed.

I felt my heart beating excitedly as I remembered the "P.S." in the Everards' letter. I wished right that second that I had the hunting rifle Barry would have with him in the car when he came. The animal was long-nosed, pointy-eared, blackish-gray, and doglike with a gray face and whitish underparts and sides. He was standing erect, and the fur on his back bristled like a dog's at Sugar Creek when it's angry about something.

"Look at that, would you!" the little man exclaimed. "It's pretty nigh two feet long and bushy as a fox's tail!"

Then Ed Wimbish startled me by blowing a

long hard blast on his horn and yelling, "Go on! Get away from that there ladder! You can't climb up there nohow! Go on! Get goin'!" He honked the horn two more short sharp blasts.

For a second, even that far away, I thought I saw the fierce-looking wolf's eyes smolder with resentment. He looked like a stubborn boy who's been interrupted by one of his parents stopping him from doing something he wanted to do and ordering him to do something he *didn't* want to do.

Then that big savage-looking monster of a timber wolf bared his fangs with his lips curled and just glared at us, as much as to say, "I hate people that interfere with what is my own business!"

When our driver raced the engine and steered us on up the lane toward the cache house, Old Timber swung himself around, looking up just once toward the top of the ladder, then trotted away lazily, as if saying, "That deer meat is not fit for a fine wolf like me." He faded away into a row of new pine like a sullen gray shadow.

My heart was still racing with excitement and maybe with a little of what Mom or Dad would call fear, but which I hoped was just plain enjoyment mixed with a little worry.

"Old Timber's been a-coming back every winter for nigh onto seven years," Ed Wimbish said. "I've tried every way possible to trap him, but he's as wary as a fox. I coulda shot him a dozen times, but Marthy won't let me do it. She wants his fur without a bullet hole in it, and she says she can't stand having him outsmart us. She says we'll get him by trap or we'll let him live. Marthy's stubborn thataway. That there's one request I want to make of you boys, and the rest of your club: don't ever shoot Old Timber! I've been having trouble with some of the farmers, and he's been shot at a half-dozen times by some of the new ranchers and hunters. But as soon as they learn how Marthy feels about it, they quit shootin'. I reckon one of these days or nights, though, Old Timber will go on a calf-killin' spree—or sheep—and he'll get a bullet."

I knew if Little Jim had been with us, or maybe Dragonfly, one of the first things he'd have said would be, "Will he eat people?" So I asked the question myself.

Old Ed answered, "Wolves around here find all they want to eat without botherin' human beings. There's plenty of deer and moose, and it's their nature to run away when approached by man. Notice how he turned tail when we got close to him?"

Right that minute our Jeep came to a jerky stop not far from a rustic lodge. A painting of a giant snow goose was above its entrance, along with large letters made from short logs of white birch, spelling out the words THE SNOW GOOSE.

Poetry and I swung into action, showing the little old-timer what good training we'd had at home. We helped him make up the beds

—I remembered exactly how I'd seen Mom do it and felt fine inside that I had learned to do it myself. Mom had seen to it that I did.

"This here's the thermostat," the trapper told us, touching it with his right forefinger. "You can have the temperature any degree you want by adjusting this. You won't need the fireplace, but it's fun to have it for roasting wieners and just to sit around with the lights off. The Everards kept it going every night. Marthy and me could look out across the lake from our house and see the flickerin' flames. Shore miss 'em a lot. But she always wanted to see Californy, so they up and left, come December."

Old Ed was gazing out across the lake toward the town of Squaw Lake, which, judging from the way it looked wasn't more than two miles away.

"It's further than four miles by the road we come on," he explained. "But in the summer, it's a shortcut to go by boat, shooting out past that neck of land that juts out and straight for our dock over there. Once in a while in the winter, when the road was blocked, me and Marthy used to snowshoe across."

Poetry's curiosity made him ask, "What's the row of evergreens doing out there in the middle of the lake? That's lake on both sides of them, isn't it?"

"That's the 'road' I was a-telling Marthy I was a-making all afternoon. I just got it finished afore I come into town to see if you'd come yet.

"That there row of evergreens runs all the

way out to the bobhouse—shanty, as I call it. See it away out there? That's where you catch the big'uns—great northern, muskies, and giant perch. The row of trees is just in case you get caught out there in a blizzard or a fog, or if you want to go out at night or come home after fishing late. You just follow the row of trees. Marthy and me pretty nigh froze once one winter when a blizzard come up while we was out there and couldn't find our way back."

My eyes followed the row of small evergreens out and out and out till they came to focus on the shanty he was talking about. I could hardly wait till we could get there and catch some of the "big'uns."

"But you can catch plenty of perch right out there, just a few feet from the second tree. Here's where the Everards keep the bait." Mr. Wimbish led us into a side room, lifted a trapdoor, and led us down an old stairway, lighting the way with his flashlight and saying as he went, "Don't know why they didn't run wires down here, but they didn't. You have to use a flashlight or a lantern or candle to see anything.

"Here's the bait box," he finished. "You'll find plenty of worms for all the perch you can catch."

"Perch?" I asked. And my tone of voice showed I thought perch were hardly worth sneezing at.

"Perch," Ed said, "is the mainstay of fishermen in the winter. Cold water doesn't bother 'em like it does bluegills and bass and crappies. Course, now and then you'll hook onto a big'un. A walleye or pickerel will bite anything, too, if you can coax 'em into it."

Back upstairs and outdoors again, old Ed, his whiskers bobbing with every word he said, pointed a long arm toward the lake. "That second tree there. That's where you'll do most of your fishing, I reckon. No use to go plumb out to the shanty in weather like this. Weather's not cold enough to need a fire or a wind shelter.

"The snow's pretty deep all around here, but it's crusted over, and you won't break through if you walk mostly in the sheltered places. That old sun's been a-bearin' down, though, last few days. Most a week now since there's been any real cold weather."

For some reason I thought then of the Everards' letter, saying Ed Wimbish himself was quite an exaggerator and to take what he said with several grains of salt. He might be a big exaggerator sometimes, I thought, but he certainly was a likeable old gentleman.

"Gotta run my trapline tomorry," he said. "Fact is, I gotta run down to the Rum River Crossin' afore dark and see if my marten traps have got anything in 'em."

Poetry and I were standing just outside the lodge door by the twin pines that sort of guarded the entrance, watching the little man buzz about, doing different things. "He's cute," Poetry's gooselike voice honked in my ear. "Look at the way he swings along."

I was watching old Ed's surefooted way of stepping. I also admired the rifle he was carrying. When he came to the cache, where he had gone to get the ladder, he stooped as if studying the tracks Old Timber had made. Then he squinted up at the heavy door and, turning around, motioned us to come out to where he was.

"I may decide to set a trap for him right here one of these days. If I do, I'll let you boys know exactly where. I wouldn't want to catch a boy. Man, look at the *size* of those tracks!"

Poetry was walking around, squinting up at the little house and studying the tracks made in the snow by the monster wolf. He had a very serious expression on his face. "I've read lots of stories about wolves, and they didn't always run away when they saw a man or boy. Sometimes they trailed 'em and—"

"Rubbish," Ed Wimbish scoffed. "Whoever wrote them stories never saw a wolf. Whoever wrote 'em maybe had read too many wolf stories by other writers who never saw a wolf, either, but had read stories by some other writer who never saw one. I've lived in these here parts for nigh onto twenty-seven years, and every wolf I ever saw was scared of me."

With that the old-timer sighed, swung his rifle into the crotch of his arm, and said, "I sure hope that Barry feller gets here tonight. If he wants to study honest-to-goodness wildlife, following the trapline with old Ed is a sure way to learn somethin'."

I knew who else would like to follow the line with him. In fact, I'd almost rather do that than catch a monster fish. Back at Sugar Creek, I'd followed Circus's trapline with him a few times, but about all he ever caught was muskrat in the fall and spring and a raccoon or a skunk now and then. Remembering that I'd always wanted to kill a bear, I asked, "Are there any bears around here?" I remembered what the Everards' letter had also said—that the bears would all be in hibernation this time of year.

"Bears?" Ed Wimbish exclaimed raspily. "That's the main reason we cache our meat up there—to keep the bears from getting it. Why, man, there's bears around here everywhere."

3

I felt a tingling sensation in my spine. My eyes looked in a quick half-worried circle of directions, expecting to see a two- or three- hundred-pound, short-legged, short-tailed, long-haired quadruped with erect ears standing on his haunches and studying us or getting ready to charge, as I'd read happening in stories.

I guess the old-timer must have thought I was really scared, because he quickly explained, "You don't need to worry. Most of 'em are asleep this time of year."

"Most of them!" I exclaimed. "I thought they *all* went into hibernation in the fall and didn't come out till spring!"

"Most of 'em do. But with the weather being warmer up here this winter, they might get restless in their beds. Last week the snow melted a little. And when it does that, sometimes water drips in on the ones that picked a log under the snow, and they come out and hunt up another hibernatin' place."

Then, because Poetry and I showed so much interest, and because there was quite a lot of firewood that had to be carried in, and we were helping him, the little trapper talked and talked and talked.

"Once last winter Marthy was a-runnin' my

37

trapline with me. Marthy's awful good on a trapline—outwalks any man I ever saw and don't lose nary a pound, neither. Fact is, she gains weight just walking through drifts for a day. She carries candy along to munch on, that's why. Well, that day Marthy accidently broke through an ice-crusted drift and plunged into a hollow under a fallen tree and landed with all her two-hundred-twenty-five-odd pounds right on a bear! And he didn't even wake up.

"She was half mad at having scratched her shins on the bark of the tree, so she whams the sleeping bruin on the nose. But he just yawned and grunted and didn't even bother to turn over. Fact is, you can turn 'em over yourself if they're *really* asleep—and if you're strong enough, of course—and they'll keep right on snoring.

"No, you don't need to be afraid. They wouldn't even be hungry—not till they've been out a while. Nature calls for almost nothing to eat for the first few days after they've waked up.

"Come spring, though, and the young'uns are with 'em, and you make 'em think they're cornered, then look out! And you can never tell when a bear *thinks* he's cornered.

"It's the mother bear you have to keep your eyes peeled for, if she has her cubs with her. I pretty nigh got mauled to death once when I accidentally got between a four-hundred-pound black bear and her two young'uns, and she thought I was a-gonna hurt 'em. She swung on me with her powerful paw, knocked me sky-west and crooked. I sure got scratched up aplenty. See that there scar there?"

Ed whisked off a mitten, pulled up his right sleeve, and showed us two scars, each eight or nine inches long. "If I hadn't had my knife out and hadn't managed to jab it into her while she was standin' over me with her hot breath a-blowin' in my face, I reckon Marthy'd have been a widow for the last three years.

"But this ain't spring, and you boys don't need to worry none."

"Did you kill her just with a hunting knife?" I asked, incredulous.

"Well now, you shouldn't of asked me that," Ed said with a twinkle in his eyes. "It sorta spoils the story. But I reckon as how, now that it's spoiled, Marthy'd expect me to tell you she saw what was a-goin' on from the window of the lodge and come a-runnin' with her .300 Magnum. Ain't nobody in these here parts can shoot straighter'n Marthy. She's kinda lost now, runnin' the store, but the doctor says she's got to quit trapline runnin' and buckin' the weather. That's why we sold the Snow Goose and moved to town—what town there is."

I was still thinking about the long scars on the old-timer's arm when I asked, "What'd you do with the bear's skin?" I'd noticed a bearskin rug on the lodge floor when we'd been inside a little while before. I hoped the bear old Ed had knifed and Marthy had shot with her .300 Magnum was the one the rug had been made of.

"We let the Everards have it when they

bought the lodge. Mrs. Everard's such a dainty little thing, and so delicate, you'd never think she'd go for something like that. But she wanted it so badly, and Marthy and her liked each other so well. Marthy's got a tender heart ever since we lost our Jerry. She's got to have something to mother, and she's spending her heart on the little Everard woman now, her and our grandniece Jeanne."

All of a sudden, Ed's voice choked, and I noticed there were tears in his gray eyes, which he brushed at with his hand, then looked away. When he looked back in our direction, I thought I read a very sad expression in them.

I knew I had when, a second later, he told us, "Marthy's had a rough time in life. She's jolly on the surface, but her heart's broke. She sort of feels that maybe there isn't any God anymore, with all her children gone. Freddie left us at thirteen. Little Marion stayed with us only till he was four, and Jerry was twenty-two and goin' to be married . . ."

The old-timer stopped abruptly and shook his head the way Little Jim does sometimes when he has tears in his eyes and wants to get them out without anybody knowing they've been there. His tone of voice changed as he said, "Well, I gotta run down the road a piece to Rum River Crossin'. I got a couple traps set for marten about a hundred yards from the last Snow Goose sign. It's quite a chore wading the snow through the underbrush, but if I could take a look at 'em, I wouldn't have to do it tomorry, maybe. There's been an Indian Devil runnin' that side of the creek, and I have to beat him to the traps, or all there is left when I get there is my traps thrown. Or if there's been any varmints in 'em, he's killed 'em and spoiled their pelts or carried them off somewhere and cached them."

"What," I asked, "is an Indian Devil?"

"A wolverine," the old-timer told us. "I've got a story a mile long to tell you about the one that's following my line. But I gotta get going now. If you want to go along—but you'd have to wait in the Jeep at the Crossin'. I could get there and back quicker alone . . ."

Poetry looked at me with his eyebrows down and a shake of his head, meaning he had a different idea and for us to stay at the lodge till Ed came back.

"I'll be back after a while." Those were the last words we were to hear the old man say for quite a spell. A lot of things were going to happen afore he got back to us'uns.

I looked out across the snowbound lake, following with my eyes the long row of evergreens all the way out to the shanty, where the fishing was the best and where we could catch some of the big'uns. I was surprised to notice how high the sun still was.

We wouldn't have time to go all the way, but we could fish awhile out by the second tree. I could hardly wait. We could have a mess of fish caught and cleaned, and when the gang got there, Poetry could have them sizzling in the pan for supper.

We'd done a little ice fishing at Sugar Creek on the bayou pond and in a few places on Sugar Creek itself, but not much—only enough to learn a little about how.

We got our tackle ready, using some we found in the lodge, because ours was with Barry and the gang somewhere back on the highway.

"We'll fish till Ed gets back," Poetry said.

As soon as we had spudded the right-size hole, we baited our hooks with the worms Mr. Wimbish had shown us and in only a few minutes were hauling in some fine yellow perch.

Just for fun we made a game of it, and Poetry said, "The next one'll be Santa Claus himself, a whopper."

And it was—a huge perch.

"My turn next," I said. "Mine's going to be a mother bear just come out of hibernation!"

And just like that—*wham!* I got a whale of a strike. I felt the line pulling and jerking down under the ice. I knew my line and leader were extrastrong, so I held on, and almost right away there was an even bigger perch flopping on the ice beside me.

While I was baiting my hook with another half-frozen worm, which acted as lazy as a sleeping bear, Poetry got a strike. I could tell by the excitement on his face that he had a really big one.

"I've got Old Timber himself!" he cried.

And before anybody could have said "Jack Robinson Crusoe," he landed a whopper of a walleye. Boy oh boy! Fishing was *really* good. *Really!* Would the gang ever be surprised!

But after that we didn't get any bites for a while, so we decided to go back to the lodge. Any minute now, the old-timer might come driving back for us.

We hadn't any sooner reached the shore than we were startled by a rabbit springing up and bounding away in a long, leaping gait. A second later, there was a grayish-brown explosion at Poetry's feet, and a covey of six partridges sailed out in a fan-shaped direction, dropping down farther on in a tangle of weeds and sedge.

I certainly felt fine. One of the happiest feelings I ever get comes from being outdoors in a woodsy place, studying wildlife signs, breathing fresh, crisp winter air—when it's not too cold—and any minute expecting to see in the snow a track of some different kind of animal. We'd already seen enough to give Barry a good start on his paper for his class.

The half-dozen partridges hadn't any sooner disappeared than I got a sad feeling in my heart, though, the sad feeling and the glad feeling getting mixed up in my mind the way they do sometimes back at Sugar Creek. I was standing and dreaming in the direction the birds had flown and at the same time looking at the chalk-white bark of a friendly little tree in front of me. It was one of my favorite trees back home—a white birch.

In the summertime at Sugar Creek, there isn't anything prettier in the whole world of trees. There is a clump of them along the marsh at the edge of a gravelly ridge, and their triangle-shaped dark green leaves are always trembling in the breeze and glistening in the sun as if they are the happiest things in the world. In the fall they are pretty, too, the leaves as yellow as the pages of the goldenrod writing tablet we use at school.

But in the wintertime, when all the leaves are gone, and all the dark blotches on the trunk just below the branches are coal black, and there isn't a single leaf left to shimmer in the breezy sunlight—well, a birch tree like the one I was looking at right that minute near the lake at Snow Goose Lodge made me feel very sorry for it. It was too bad, I thought, that there had to be such a thing as freezing weather to kill all the leaves, and cold driving winds to blow them from their summer home on the tree and whirl them away into nothing.

We moseyed along away from the shore, looking for other signs of wildlife, expecting any second we might scare up a snowshoe rabbit or flush another covey of partridges.

All of a sudden Poetry stopped and exclaimed, "Listen! I hear water running!"

I stopped and listened and *did* hear water, like a small stream gurgling. It took us only another minute to find a singing brook, completely covered with snow and ice except for here and there where a patch of dark water hissed and tumbled over rocks.

"It's like the branch back at Sugar Creek," I said. "Water flows *under* the ice."

We followed the stream to its mouth, which was at the lake itself. There was quite a patch of open water there, so clear you could see the bottom.

We stayed only a few minutes and were wandering on back toward the lodge, both of us feeling fine and glad to be alive, when all of a sudden Poetry's voice honked into my peace of mind. "William Jasper Collins!" he cried. "Stop dragging my walleye in the snow!"

I certainly hadn't realized I was doing it—I was carrying the whole stringer of fish. His interruption was so startling, blasting into my thoughts, that it stirred up my sleeping temper. Without knowing I was going to do it, I gave the stringer a disgusted toss in the direction of the lake, where it landed at the base of the sad little white birch tree.

The half-dozen perch and the walleye hadn't any sooner landed than there was a shadow of excited wings from somewhere up in the air. With a harsh, rattling cry, something swooped down toward the stringer of fish and landed with a flapping-winged *sizzlety-plop* right on them. There was an excited flurry of feathers then and some fast action, and a crested black-and-blue-and-white bird, which looked about twelve inches long, was in the air, flying like a

Sugar Creek blue jay straight for his perch high in the dead branches of a cottonwood.

Poetry came to life in a flurry of temper and angry words. He yelled up at the bird on the bare, gray treetop, "You come back here with that fish! I worked hard to catch that!"

He scooped up a snowball to throw, but I stopped him, saying, "That's a kingfisher! Let him have one little fish. He's hungry!"

Talk about a lot of ridiculous motions. That kingfisher certainly was going through the most twisted-up contortions you ever saw a bird go through, trying to keep his balance on the branch and at the same time swallow one of our medium-sized perch completely whole.

Here was more help for Barry. I could tell him about the perch and also what I already knew about kingfishers from having learned it back home. I never in my life saw a saucier bird. The kingfisher is as noisy around his house as a whole neighborhood of robins. A pair of them make their home in the bluff near the Sugar Creek bridge. Most of the time, when the kingfisher isn't way back in his hole in the bluff, he's perched on a tree stump above the creek, watching his chance to swoop down into the water for a fish. That is his only food, except for crawfish and frogs and sometimes, when fishing is bad, a few locusts and beetles. And he always tries to swallow completely whole whatever he gets.

Once, back at Sugar Creek, we'd dug back into a kingfisher's hole in a sandbank. When we finally found his nest, we saw it was made of small pellets of fish bones and shells of craw-fish. After he'd digested the fish, he'd swallowed the bones and shells backward and made a nest of them.

And talk about a noisy family! The kingfisher and his kingfisher wife and their kingfisher children scream and shriek at each other as if they didn't have a peaceful thought in their large, long-crested heads.

Sometimes, when there was a mild, open winter back at Sugar Creek, two or three king-fishers would stay all winter, not bothering to make the long, tiresome migration to a warmer climate where fishing might be better.

It was easy to see that this saucy bird that had swooped down out of nowhere and stolen one of our perch would be tempted to stay in the North—just as the bears would have a hard time staying asleep in such nice weather. He could probably catch plenty of small fish in the water at the mouth of the little stream.

Well, it took that clown of a kingfisher only about three minutes to beat that perch into being quiet and to gulp him down. Then he shook his feathers, wiped his sharp, straight, longer-than-his-head bill on the bare dead branch he was on, and swallowed three or four times as if maybe there was a part of the perch's tail that wasn't all the way down. A flash of a second later, he took off with a rattling shriek in the direction of a low bank about fifty yards up the lake, where I saw him light and disappear into a hole the size of a rabbit's burrow.

Poetry picked up our stringer of fish and said, "Come on, let's get these to the lodge before some other wild animal with wings comes galloping down from the sky and steals all the rest of them!"

"Don't begrudge a friendly, lonely fisherman one little fish!" I said.

"It wasn't so *little!*" Poetry exclaimed. "That was *my* fish! I don't catch *small* fish!"

As we ambled toward the lodge, for a while we pretended to quarrel over whose fish had been stolen. It was getting later fast, and I knew pretty soon it'd be sundown. Ed Wimbish hadn't come back yet, and the gang would have to step on the gas to get here before dark.

Our friendly quarrel was interrupted by Poetry letting out a whoop. "There they are! Coming around the bend! Oh boy! Will they ever think I *really* caught a fish!"

There was a wild honking of Barry's car coming from the other side of the cache where we'd first seen Old Timber. In minutes they were swinging around the bend in the trail and coming to a stop in a flurry of snow not more than ten feet from the twin pines at the door of the lodge.

Quicker than anything the car doors were open, and what looked like a whole swarm of boys came catapulting out.

Barry Boyland was not only going to get a chance to study wildlife in the frozen North but was going to have to do something about taming down some of it—six two-legged animals that exploded into the wildest lot of whoops and hollers and actions you ever heard six boys explode into in your life!

"Look here!" Dragonfly cried, calling from over near the outdoor cache, where a little more than two hours ago Poetry and I had seen Old Timber, maybe the biggest wolf there ever was. "Here's a *bear's* tracks! There's a *bear* around here somewhere!"

Poetry looked at me and winked and kept still, and I winked back at him and kept still, waiting to see what the rest of the gang would say when they saw the huge doglike tracks in the snow.

Circus got to where Dragonfly was first and let out an explosive groan. "*Dog* tracks!" he exclaimed. "Somebody's big hound's been around here."

Well, there wasn't any reason we shouldn't tell the rest of the gang what had really made the tracks, so Poetry and I helped each other tell the exciting story of how, while we had been in the Jeep with Ed Wimbish, we had seen the biggest wolf there ever was in "these here parts." And that Ed didn't want anybody to shoot him, because he and Marthy wanted to outsmart him by catching him in a trap.

I looked around at all the faces of the gang to see if anybody was going to be afraid of the big bad wolf, and it looked as if quite a few of us were—nearly all of us, in fact, except maybe

Theodore Collins's only son, who was only a little bit worried. I *was* wondering, though, if Ed Wimbish was right and that wolves were cowards and didn't like to eat people and wouldn't unless they were starved half to death.

The gang was in a mischievous mood for a while, and different ones of us quoted to the rest of us some of the lines of an old story we'd had in one of our Sugar Creek School readers, "The Old Wolf and the Three Little Pigs."

"Little pig! Little pig! Let me come in!" Poetry cried and raced over to the oak door of the Snow Goose and began to pound on it.

Circus called back in what he tried to make sound like a pig's squealing voice, saying, "Not by the hair of my chinny-chin-chin!"

With that, Little Jim piped up in the best growl he could manage, "Then I'll huff and I'll puff and I'll blow your house in."

Barry broke into our fun almost right away to say, "How about all of you huffing and puffing on that rick of fireplace wood over there so we'll be sure to have enough for tonight and tomorrow."

In a little while we were huffing and puffing louder than we needed to, carrying logs of oak and ash and pine and balm of Gilead and stacking them in a large stack in the fuel room of the lodge.

There was a lot of excitement over the string of fish Poetry and I had caught, and most of the gang wanted to go out onto the lake right away to catch some more. But because it was already twilight, Barry said, "No. We'd better clean the few we have and make our supper."

Tomorrow would be the big day—the *actual* beginning of our vacation, I thought—not knowing that the first exciting experience would start even sooner.

Evening came in a hurry, and we all scrambled around, getting supper and laughing and talking and helping Barry and ourselves decide which bunks were to be whose and getting our luggage unpacked. Boy oh boy! A winter vacation studying wildlife in the frozen North!

I was glad to notice Barry's rifle was in the corner, where it would be handy in case some of the wildlife we had come up to study decided it wanted to see how good a *boy* would taste for breakfast or dinner or supper or a midnight snack.

Poetry and I were busy at the sink by the iron pump when, all of a sudden, Dragonfly broke into the half silence with a hissing exclamation, saying, "Listen, everybody! There's something scratching at the door!"

I started, my fish scaler in my right hand. My hair began to crawl under my hat, which, even though we were inside the lodge, was still on. There *was* something at the door. Then I heard something else—an animal voice like a wildcat's growl.

My mind's eye visualized a brownish-gray bobtailed lynx, which I'd read there were in the North country. In fact, I'd read as much as

I could in our school library and in the Collins library upstairs in our Sugar Creek house about all the different kinds of wildlife up here. I wanted to be as much help to Barry as possible during our vacation.

Barry shushed us all and quick got his flash camera ready, just in case there would be a chance for a picture of a real-life wild animal for the paper he was going to write.

Again there was the scratching at the door, and then a bumping noise against the window just above the sink where Poetry and I were cleaning the fish. And then my hair did start to do strange things under my cap. For the length of a firefly's fleeting flash I'd seen—not a few yards away on the snowy ground but right on the windowsill itself—a moving blur of grayish-brown, tigerlike fur and sharp claws clinging to the sill. And then it was gone.

Quick as a flash, Barry was at the door. "I want a shot at whatever it is," he exclaimed.

The very second that door was open, there was a streak of grayish-brown, and something that at first looked three feet long dashed in. It leaped onto the worktable, where there were three yellow perch lying waiting to be cleaned. It seized one of them in its mouth, jumped down onto the floor, scooted under the writing desk by the window, and started eating that perch headfirst.

"It's a *house cat!*" Little Jim cried excitedly, his eyes shining. "A great big tomcat house cat!"

It was disappointing. Even though I'd been startled into a scared feeling, afraid it *was* some kind of fierce wild animal, and was glad it wasn't, yet I was sorry it wasn't.

That big beautiful tiger cat wasn't going to get by with eating my perch, I thought. As I'd done many a time back home when Mixy had stolen one of my smaller sunfish or chubs, I started toward the writing desk.

"Stop!" Poetry cried to me, seizing my arm. "Let him have it. That's the one I caught. It was just before the walleye on the stringer."

I don't know how I happened to be as bright as I was right then, but for some reason I thought to say, "OK, chum, your choice. That's two of yours stolen—one for the kingfisher, one for the cat, and *none* for the little boy who's already too fat."

Little Jim, who was always ready to help anybody have fun, piped up with a few lines of a poem.

> "Baa, baa, black sheep, have you any
> wool?
> Yes sir, yes sir, three bags full—
> One for my master, and one for my
> dame,
> And one for the little boy who lives in
> the lane."

Everybody was in a good humor, even the big tiger house cat, still under the writing desk, still eating Poetry's perch.

Dragonfly, who was over by the window looking out through a place in the frosted glass, spoke then, saying, "How'd anybody get a row of evergreens to grow in the middle of that lake, if that *is* a lake out there?"

I knew he was wondering as I had wondered when I'd first seen the row of evergreens—spruce or fir, I wasn't sure which—starting at the place where we'd caught our fish and stretching away into the distance like a row of green soldiers marching.

"That," I said loftily to Dragonfly, "is a 'road.'"

"A road?" he asked, astonished.

"Yes, a road. Of course, if you were good in grammar, you'd know the word 'road' has quotation marks around it. Mr. Wimbish set the evergreens there in the ice and snow to mark the way out to the shanty where the fishing is best. If there's a fog or a blizzard, or if you go at night, all you have to do is follow the row of trees and you can find it. Or if you're *out* there when it's foggy or blizzardy, you can find your way back."

It had been fun for Poetry and me to spud our own fishing hole in the afternoon. It'd be still more fun tomorrow to go out to the shanty—the "bobhouse," as Mr. Wimbish had called it—to try for my whopper walleye or great northern. Or maybe I'd catch a monster muskie to have mounted and placed on the wall of my room back home, where everybody could see it and be reminded of what a good fisherman I was.

"I wanted to go fishing *tonight!*" Dragonfly said.

And so did several of the rest of us.

"It's early to bed tonight," Barry ordered from the stove, where he and Poetry—Poetry wearing a high, white chef's hat to make him look like a cook—were busy with the fish fillets and other things we had to eat.

"I won't be sleepy," Dragonfly whined.

"You will be in the morning," Barry said. And his tone of voice said that was the end of the argument. And it was, because he added in the same tone of voice, "We'll make our first trip out in the *daytime.*"

"Dinner's ready," Poetry sang out.

He was answered by Circus, who hardly ever made any cute remarks but this time did, saying, "Little Tommy Tucker sang for his *supper,* not his *dinner.* Imagine the poem going: 'Little Tommy Tinner sang for his dinner.'"

But it didn't matter which it was, supper or dinner. It was something for six hungry boys and their camp director to eat. In a little while we were seated around the table under the big light hanging from the rafter. Little Jim, in a mischievous mood, looked at the six fish on the large platter in the center of the table and said, "One for the kingfisher, one for the cat, and *none* for the little boy who is already too fat."

It was time for the blessing, which we always had, even when we were out in the woods. We never knew which kind it would be, though—

somebody being called on to actually pray with his voice, or if it would be what at our house we call a "Quaker blessing," when each one bows his head and *thinks* his prayer to God, instead of speaking it in a whisper or an actual voice.

My own thoughts were about Mom and Dad and Charlotte Ann, who right that very minute were probably at the table in our kitchen, and Dad was saying, "Bless our son up there in the frozen North. Protect him from harm. Help him to remember whose boy he is —ours. Help him to *think* and help him grow into a strong, fine, clean young man who will be an honor to Your name and to the *family* name . . ."

I knew he would pray a prayer something like that, because I'd heard him pray it every time just before I'd gone on a vacation anywhere without him and Mom.

While not a one of us was saying a word, and all we could hear was tomcat chewing perch bones under the writing desk, all of a sudden there was the sound of a car engine not far from the lodge. It backfired every few seconds, and I knew it was the old-timer himself come back from looking at his marten traps.

Right away there was a wild honking of his horn, reminding me of the time I'd heard him honk it to scare Old Timber away from the cache ladder.

Then I heard Ed Wimbish's raspy voice coming through the twilight, saying, "I told you before! Get away from that ladder!"

And then I heard another explosive noise —and it wasn't from his oldish Jeep backfiring. It was like a *gun* firing!

Had Old Ed lost his patience? Had he changed his mind about catching the big bad wolf in a trap and had shot him instead?

4

Imagine that! Just when you are in the middle of the beginning of your vacation in the frozen North, where you are going to help your camp director study wildlife, while you are sitting quietly at the supper table asking a Quaker blessing on the fish and other food you're going to have—and while you are getting hungrier every second—imagine what an explosion there is in your mind when, right in the middle of all that quiet, you are half-scared out of what few wits you have by an ear-deafening blast from a gun just outside the big oak door behind you! Then you hear running steps and know that, any second, whoever is out there will come bursting into the lodge!

I jumped as if I had been shot at and missed. Then I felt excitement whirling all around me as there was a whamming against the door itself and a voice—the rasping, excited voice of Ed Wimbish—calling, "Let me in, quick!"

The word "quick" was a squeaky cry like that of an animal caught in a trap and badly hurt.

Since the door was directly behind me, I not only jumped as if I had been shot at and missed but also as if I had been hit. I was up and starting to shove my chair back out of the way so I could get to the door.

At the same time, several of the rest of the gang were doing the same thing. In a fourth of a minute, three of us were in a football pileup in front of the door. It took Barry a little while to get us out of the way and finally open the door.

With the wiry, excited little man as he whizzed in came the odor of gun smoke and another odor a little like that of polecat, only not nearly so strong. Ed carried a game sack with something inside. I'd seen a sack like that many a time back home when we'd been hunting and had shot a rabbit or several and were carrying them home.

Mr. Wimbish started talking the minute he got in, his eyes blinking a little at the light. "The ornery critter's a-gettin' more daring every day. Must thought I was a-bringin' him his supper. Why, the varmint wasn't more'n twenty feet from me when I opened the car door! One of these days or nights I'm a-gonna lose my temper and my good sense and shoot straight at him. If I don't quit shootin' over his head, he'll get a notion I cain't shoot straight and there aren't nothin' to be afraid of, and I'll come home some night and find him with my grandmother's nightgown on in bed a-waitin' to eat me up!"

There was plenty of excitement for a while as old Ed told his story. He'd stopped at two of his marten traps, and both had had the triggers pulled. One of them also had a marten in it, dead as a doornail under the deadfall log.

"The other trap had been sprung, too, but there weren't a thing under it. Fact is, there weren't any log anywhere near the place. Some ornery varmint had helped himself to my fish-head bait. The slickest critter I ever smelt. And I mean *smelt!* And he musta had a temper a mile long. My stake enclosure was like a house after a tornado had struck it. The log was scratched and gnawed and dragged a dozen feet through the trees, and there was a musky odor all over everything. I reckon we're goin' to have half our traps throwed or broken to-morry. Once a wolverine gets started, he never knows when to quit."

Our tiger house cat had finished his perch quite a while ago and acted still hungry. He was sniffing around Ed's gunnysack now.

We were all talking, asking questions and making remarks, and I was enjoying a whole new boys' world I'd never been in before, listening and learning and feeling fine. But I was also feeling sorry for the beautiful glossy-black marten old Ed very proudly brought from the gunnysack and stretched out on the floor for us to see.

"Here, Tiger," he said to the tomcat. "Want to see a *black* cat?"

It seemed Tiger did, but, as cats do, he only sniffed at it a little and turned away. Then he mewed lazily and rubbed his sleek fat sides against Little Jim's legs.

Ed explained, as we crowded around with a lot more curiosity than the cat had, "This is a *rare* marten or a 'fisher' as some folks call 'em. This one's all black and worth a lot of money. A *lot* of it. You hardly ever get one that's all black. We call 'em 'black cats' or, sometimes, 'black foxes.'"

All of a sudden, old Ed looked up from admiring the very beautiful long-bodied, black-tailed, short-legged, pointy-muzzled "black cat" and exclaimed, "Marthy'll be worried to death. I forgot to tell her I was a-gonna run them two traps afore supper. You be ready at four in the morning, and we'll take off for the whole line. How many of you a-goin'?" he finished.

Barry didn't know how many or which ones of us were going to go on the first trapline trip, but we'd decide before four in the morning, he told the little old gentleman.

Right away, as happy with his marten as Charlotte Ann with a new doll, Ed was out the door and gone with his gunnysack with the high-priced marten, or "black cat," or fisher in it. He said as he left, and as the light from our cabin cast a shadow ahead of him in the snow, "Sure's a warm night for January. Never seen it so warm in the winter afore."

A few seconds later, his Jeep came to clattering life, and he was off in a noisy hurry up the lane on his way to his Marthy—Marthy, who was good at following traplines, too, and who once had stepped on a live sleeping bear, when she had broken through a drift into his hibernating place.

Barry was getting quite a lot of material for his important paper. Already he could write about seven perch, one walleye, a rattling-voiced kingfisher that made his home in the bank up the lake, a nest of partridges, a huge timber wolf that was "the biggest ever seen in these here parts," and a twenty-pound marten out of which furriers could make sable furs for some woman somewhere to pay for. Also he could write in his paper something about a musky-smelling glutton of a wolverine that was spoiling old Ed's trapline.

Big Jim washed the dishes, and, because Little Jim begged to dry them, the rest of us let him, not feeling very sad that we didn't get to do it ourselves.

Barry was over at the writing desk typing for a while and writing in a notebook with his pencil. Once as I passed by him on my way to lie down on the bearskin rug in front of the screened fireplace, I sort of accidentally saw a few words of what he had written. The very second I saw what I saw, I realized it wasn't any boy's business, and I hurried past. The words stuck in my mind, though. His writing, as far as I read, said:

Dear Jeanne:

Looking forward to next June. Can hardly wait till you come next weekend. Bring your snowshoes and ski outfit. The boys'll love you, as "others" do and can't help "themselves." Will have this postmarked at Forty Mile Crossing tomorrow . . .

Because we had to get up early to go with the old-timer on his trapline run, we all went to bed early. Still, we were a pretty groggy bunch when Barry routed us out at four in the morning, but we took it as cheerfully as we could, Poetry starting his day by a short verse from Robert Louis Stevenson, which went:

In winter, I get up at night
And dress by yellow candlelight;
In summer, quite the other way—
I have to go to bed by day.

Again it was a surprisingly warm day, and we had a wonderful time. Barry took enough notes and pictures of different kinds of wildlife to give him many pages of material for his paper. I also discovered a lot of muscle I didn't know I had. When we dragged ourselves into bed that night, I thought I'd never been so tired in my half-long life—as also did all of us.

We had our first experience fishing in an ice shanty the next morning. It was another sunshiny day, surprisingly warm. Right after breakfast we got our tackle ready and a can of night crawlers from the basement and started out across the lake, following the road of evergreens. One of the first things I noticed as we rambled along was that each tree had a lot of snow piled up around the base. Marks of Ed's shovel still showed where he had used the back of it to pack the snow good and tight around each tree's small trunk.

"That's so the wind won't blow the trees away on a stormy day or night, I'll bet," Little Jim's bright little mind thought to say.

Big Jim tested with his boot the cone-shaped pile of snow around one of the trees and said, "The snow was wet when he packed it. Now it's ice."

Barry had let us go on ahead without him. He wanted to do a little writing on his paper. "I can think better alone," he told us—maybe meaning we were too noisy.

The traction-grip tire tracks of old Ed's Jeep were so clean in some places that you could actually see the sharp corners of their six-sided studs. He'd probably loaded the Jeep with the trees and driven them right out across the lake, stopping every so often to set one out.

When we finally reached the shanty, which was at least a mile from the lodge, and maybe a lot farther—it was hard to judge distances on a snow-covered lake—Little Jim looked toward the east in the direction of Squaw Lake town, shading his eyes against the sun and said, "There aren't any tire tracks on *that* road. Where does that go?"

The road he was talking about was another row of evergreens, leading off at a right angle from the one we'd come on and stretching away for a mile or so to a cabin or cottage hidden among the pines. Blue smoke rose lazily from a chimney, meaning somebody lived there.

"I'll bet that's where Ed and Martha live,"

Poetry suggested to me. "They made a 'road' out there too."

The ice shanty was the very first I'd ever been in, and I could hardly wait till we had unlatched the door and were inside in the half-dark. One of the first things I noticed was a kerosene lantern on a shelf on one of the walls. "That's to see with when anybody fishes at night," Circus suggested. And it probably was.

Beside the lantern I saw a box of safety matches, one of which Big Jim used to start a fire in an old-fashioned iron stove. We used kindling that was already in it and put in a few logs of wood from a stack along the wall. I'd noticed there was quite a large rick of the same kind of wood just outside also.

"The old man's a pretty good carpenter," Big Jim said. His father built houses, and Big Jim would know about those things. The floor of the house was made of boards an inch thick, with two trapdoors through which we were supposed to fish. Each trapdoor was a foot and a half square. When we lifted them up, they could be leaned back against the wall.

"That's so they won't get stumbled over if you have a big fish on and get excited and step into the water and get yourself all wet, I'll bet," Little Jim guessed in a cheerful voice.

"The head of the class for you," Poetry answered, showing he had probably thought of the same thing but knew that he hadn't thought to say it first.

The walls of the house were made of plywood, covered on the outside with tar paper so that they would be windproof and it'd be easy to keep the house warm on an extracold day or night.

The whole house was maybe eight by ten feet, plenty big for all of us to fish in and not be too crowded. Some of us had to stoop a little to get in the door, though. Circus and Big Jim had to, since they were the tallest. There was also a high sill we had to step over.

"What's the high sill for?" Dragonfly whined. He had stumbled over it when he came in and landed with a *whammety-thud* on the floor.

"To keep cold drafts off your feet," Big Jim answered, "and also to keep snow from blowing in on a windy day when the door's open. And to keep water from running in if the snow melts outside." What he said was probably right, I thought.

There were four small windows, one of them just above the door and having a blind that could be drawn.

Poetry guessed what the blind was for—also what the sliding wooden covers at the other windows were for. "It's so, if you're fishing in the daytime, you can shut out the light. Then you can see fish swimming around and they can't see you, and you can watch them biting."

There were benches, built so they could be folded down against the wall, and above them was an extrawide shelf, just high enough so that your head didn't touch it when you were sitting on the bench.

"Well, what do you know about that?" I exclaimed. I'd seen another shelf with a little camp cooking stove on it and a first-aid kit and a few other supplies that freezing wouldn't hurt.

"And look!" Dragonfly said. "There are some blankets on the high shelf. If we get cold or the fire goes out, we can wrap up in 'em and keep warm!"

"They're for staying all night, if you want to sleep here, I'll bet," Little Jim put in. "And that high shelf is wide enough to be the upper berth of a bunk bed."

Pretty soon we were ready to fish, and pretty soon we were doing it, having the shanty as dark as we could make it and still have ventilation. We used both holes under the two trapdoors, having to spud new ones, though, because the weather had been colder since the last person or persons had fished here, and the surface had frozen over.

Ice fishing in a shanty wasn't as much fun as fishing from a boat in warm weather, but we did enjoy it, especially when every now and then one of us would get a whopper on and actually land it.

We had a couple two-or-three-pound walleyes and about six perch before we heard somebody coming.

"It's Barry, I'll bet," Circus said. "Just listen to the song he's whistling."

I listened, as did we all, and the melody was one I'd heard quite a few times at *weddings* back at Sugar Creek. Circus, the best singer of the gang and knowing a lot of songs by heart, started singing the words, the first few of which are:

> Because you come to me, with naught
> save love, dear . . .

"Poor Barry!" Poetry said sadly, cutting in on Circus.

"She's pretty, though," I said. Poetry and I were the only ones of the gang to have seen her, when we were under the potted palm in the lobby of the hotel back in Minneapolis.

"Yeah, but she looks citified," he countered. "Barry ought to have a girl who can rough it. I'll bet she'd be as helpless as a kitten on a camping trip. Why—"

"*Sh!*" Big Jim chopped Poetry's sentence off at its very beginning. "Don't let him hear you!"

Barry was just outside the door, so that ended our talk about him and the kind of helpless, extrapretty, dainty girl he was going to marry next June, and who, the last of the week, was going to drive Barry's station wagon up from Minneapolis. As you already know, we'd borrowed her car for most of the gang to drive up in.

Barry's coming ended our talk, but it didn't end our worries. It seemed all right for our camp director to have a special friend, and we supposed he had a right to get married, but what *would* we do for a camp director next time we wanted to come up here or go to some other place on a vacation? Barry wouldn't belong to our boys' world anymore but would be living in a married people's world, which seemed to have a high wall separating it from *our* world.

Barry stopped whistling when he reached the shanty door. He knocked a cheerful knock and called out, "Little pig, little pig! Let me come in!"

Big Jim, who had an almost mustache on his upper lip, answered, "Not by the fuzz under my nosey-nose-nose."

Well, we caught a few more medium-sized fish. Then all of us went back to camp, cleaned them, and took a drive in the Jeep with old Ed to see different winter scenes.

The days flew by too fast, and the weather kept on being what they called unseasonably warm. We liked the warmer weather, but it wasn't best for fur, Ed said. He didn't want nature to decide spring was here, and the "varmints" begin to shed, and their fur be worth a lot less.

Every day Barry worked on his special paper, and we had plenty of time for ourselves to do as we wished, except that we had to stay close to camp unless when Barry or the old-timer was with us.

We still hadn't caught any *real* whoppers, and we hadn't seen many large animals—only a few deer and once a red fox. Old Timber seemed to have left the country, as if he didn't like human beings and the deer meat in the cache wasn't fit for a fine wolf like him.

Too soon our vacation would be over. Too soon the girl who next June was going to rob us of our camp director would come driving up in the station wagon. "She may be the helpless type," Big Jim said to us once when we were out by the kingfisher's tree, "but we're going to be polite and courteous and show her that the Sugar Creek Gang knows how to treat a lady."

We voted on it, and the count was six to nothing in favor of acting as if we were pleased half to death that there was going to be a wedding in June.

Along toward the last of our week, the old-timer decided to run his trapline again. This time it was to be a fast trip, so he and Barry would go alone. The littlest ones of us would slow down the hike too much. We were to stay near camp and not let ourselves get out of sight of it.

As they had the day of the first trip, Barry and Ed started about four in the morning. I hardly woke up at all when the lights of the four-wheel-drive Jeep pickup came shining down the lane and into the lodge windows.

It felt good not to have to get up, even though the smell of frying bacon and eggs made my mouth water. I was glad I could sleep a while longer, and when I did get up, I could dress by good old yellow sunlight.

The noise of the Jeep outside the open door almost drowned out Barry's last words to Big Jim, which were: "We'll try to be back by noon, but we're hoping to spot a deer. If we do, we'll do a little stalking. I need a camera shot of one close up. If we *don't* get back by noon, don't worry. You know how to cook. Better not get too far from camp. Be sure you can always see the Snow Goose sign from wherever you are. Get it?"

"Got it!" several of our voices grunted.

I went to sleep again, hearing the Jeep engine fade away down the lane.

It was quite late by the time we all had waked up, had our breakfast, and were ready for the day—our next to the last one before Ed and Marthy's grandniece would come with the station wagon.

The first thing I noticed when we stepped out into the morning was that there had been a fresh snowfall during the night. The sun was shining again, though, and it was going to be an even warmer day than some of the warmest we had had.

Water was already dripping off the roof. The new snow up there was melting because of the sunshine and the higher temperature.

The first thing Dragonfly did was make a beeline for the ladder leading up to the cache, where a second later he yelled back to us, "Come here, you guys! There's been some man running around here barefooted!"

5

We were used to Dragonfly yelling crazy things for us to come and see. The very first day we'd been there, as you know, he'd yelled that there were bear tracks around the cache ladder, when it had been only those of Old Timber. So nobody paid any attention to him this time.

But Dragonfly's voice sounded very insistent. He kept on yelling to us, "But there's a bare-foot man's tracks here! All around the place!"

"Wolf!" Circus yelled back.

"Wolf!" several of the rest of us echoed.

But Dragonfly wouldn't give up. "They're seven times as big as a wolf's tracks! Come and see for yourselves!"

"Might as well humor him," Poetry grunted to me, stopping winding the handline he had been getting ready for fishing.

He sauntered with me through the new snow over to where Dragonfly was.

Circus must have gotten the same idea as Poetry, because he got there at the same time. He hadn't any sooner glimpsed what Dragonfly had been looking at for quite a while than he let out a whistle that seemed to say, "What on earth!" With his voice, he called out to the rest of the gang, "It *might* be a bear!"

"It can't be," Big Jim called from where he was, also on the way to us. "Bears are in hibernation now and won't come out till spring."

I didn't say anything, but I was remembering what the old-timer had told us the first of the week. Sometimes a bear's winter sleeping quarters get uncomfortable for him, due maybe to warm weather and melting snow, and he comes out. The footprints did look almost exactly like those of a very large, barefoot man. Not a claw print was visible. I knew enough from what I'd looked up about animals before I'd left home that if it *was* a bear, the tracks of the back feet would look a lot like those of a barefoot man, but those of the front feet would be different.

I said so to the gang, and Dragonfly pouted an answer, saying, "That's why I know it's a man! All the tracks are alike. There aren't any front-feet tracks!"

And he was right. All the tracks around the cache *were* like those of a barefoot man. Each one had five toe prints.

We stopped and looked into each other's eyes. It *couldn't* be a bear, because bears were in hibernation—or were supposed to be—but how on earth could it have been a man? Why would anybody want to go barefoot in the snow in the winter?

I was surprised at Little Jim, who decided it for us. He said, "If it was a man, his *big* toe would be on *one* side and the *little* toe on the other. See? This track's got two little toes, one

73

on each side, and one big toe right in the *middle!*"

And I saw that he was right. Not only that, but a second later, about ten feet from the cache in the direction of the white birch, where on our first afternoon I'd tossed our stringer of fish, Circus spotted the animal's front-feet tracks. They had five toes, too, but at the end of each toe print was the mark of a long claw. The rest of the track looked exactly like that of a big five-toed dog, except that a dog track would have only *four* toes.

Big Jim spoke then, saying, "He was standing on his hind feet back there, looking up at the cache and wishing there was some way he could get up. Here, he's walking on all *four* feet!"

Well, that settled it. There was a bear around here somewhere. Something had waked him from his winter's nap—the warm weather, maybe.

"Let's trail him to see where he went," Poetry suggested. Pretending to be a hound, he let out a long bawl like Circus's pop's old black-and-tan on a coon trail at night along the Sugar Creek bayou. Right away the rest of us, whooping it up like five other hounds, were right after him. That is, I *thought* all the rest of us were.

When we got stopped by Big Jim ordering us to stop, I knew there'd been only five of us on the trail.

Big Jim said, "The forest is pretty dense all

around here, and we can't run any risk of getting lost or getting clawed or mauled by a bear. It'd be the easiest thing in the world to get lost out there somewhere. Besides, I promised Barry we'd stay close to camp."

I took a sad look out across an open space leading to a thicket of evergreens toward which the bear's tracks led. My heart was pounding with excitement for wanting to actually see the bear. I complained a little to Big Jim, saying, "For the first few days after a bear wakes up out of hibernation, nature calls for only a little food, just *a little*." I was quoting Ed Wimbish.

"How do you know he's been awake only a few days?" Big Jim countered. "Wasn't he hungry enough to stand on his hind legs and lick his chops in the direction of the deer meat up there?"

Still not liking to have my desires squelched, I said, "All right, then. Let's go fishing and have fish for dinner. Let's go out to the shanty and catch some big ones."

But we decided not to go *before* dinner. It was a long way out there, and we could probably catch quite a few near the second tree at the beginning of the tree road anyway—which we did. Big Jim decided *that* for us, too.

That squelched two of my ideas. I had wanted to trail the bear and hadn't gotten to. I'd wanted to follow the evergreen road away out to the shanty and catch some really big fish and hadn't gotten to. I felt sort of surly in my mind. I shouldn't have, because anybody with good sense could see that Big Jim was right, but for a while I didn't have the good sense that I knew I should have.

All the time we were catching medium and baby-sized yellow perch, I was smoldering inside. I kept thinking about the bear, wishing we could see him before he found a new hibernating place and went back to sleep for the rest of the winter.

Poetry must have been thinking the same thing. When he and I were alone for a little while, he said to me, "I wonder where he was holed up *before* the warm weather spoiled his hiding place."

Well, Poetry and Little Jim and I found out that very morning. The rest of the gang wasn't with us at the time, and it happened kind of accidentally.

When we got back to the shore with our string of all perch—not a single walleye or northern or bass or muskie among them—we spotted the kingfisher high on his dead tree, watching for a chance to swoop down with a harsh, rattling cry onto our stringer, seize a fish lunch—or dinner—and fly back with it, go through a dozen acrobatic stunts swallowing it whole, and then shoot home to his hole in the bank a hundred yards up the shore.

I was carrying the stringer of perch at the time, so when Poetry said, "It's your turn to feed the kingfisher. Give him one of the ones you caught," I took him up on the idea. I selected one of the smaller fish that would be just about the right size for one bite for a kingfisher, tore it off the stringer, and handed the stringer to Big Jim. Then when we got to the white birch tree, I tossed the perch on the ground.

Talk about action! Almost before I could have said, "Scat!" there was a flash of black-and-blue-and-white dropping like a bullet from the dead branch down onto the dead perch by the birch. With a flash of fluttering wings and rattling voice, the kingfisher was up and away. This time, though, instead of flying up to his tree to eat his perch, he raced off across the sky to his den.

It happened so quickly that not a one of the rest of the gang except Little Jim had seen it. The others were almost all the way to the lodge at the time.

"Come on!" Poetry said to Little Jim and me. "Let's go see where he lives!"

It was a good idea. We had to work our way through underbrush and new tree growth, around a few snow-covered rocks, and then through deep drifts, which, because of the warmer weather had had the crust melted on the surface. We kept breaking through, making it hard going.

Finally, quite a ways from the lodge, we came to a fallen tree that had broken off about six feet from the ground. Part of the trunk was still fastened to the stump. The snow had piled up in a huge drift all along the length of the trunk. It was a very large pine tree.

I was remembering the old-timer's story

about how Marthy had accidentally slipped off a log into a drift and broken through and landed on a sleeping bear underneath, so I climbed up onto that long tree trunk, crying to Poetry and to Little Jim, "Follow the leader!"

Follow the leader they did. But Little Jim, being nearer to the stump than I, clambered up quick and got ahead of Poetry and me. He was crying with his own excited, mischievous voice, pleased at the trick he had played on me, "Follow the leader!" And away he went like a little chipmunk, scampering along the trunk toward the place where it was broken halfway off the stump.

Poetry and I were panting along after him, balancing ourselves on the tree trunk and feeling wonderful when all of a sudden Little Jim let out a happy scream, poised as if he was on a diving board, held his nose, and yelled, "Here I come!" Then he jumped, not headfirst as a boy does sometimes but straight out so that he could land on his feet.

He landed on his feet all right, but the snowdrift's crust was thin because of the warmer weather they'd been having up here. The little guy broke through and went down. And I mean *down*. In any ordinary drift, a boy his weight would have sunk in only a foot or so, at least not any deeper than up to his hips.

Right then I was about to lose my balance. So while I was struggling to keep from falling off the tree trunk, I didn't see just how far Little Jim had sunk in. When my eyes came back to look for him, he wasn't there! He'd completely disappeared.

What on earth! In a snowdrift?

But by the time I got there, with Poetry right behind me, Little Jim was yelling happily, "Bill! Poetry! Come here! It's a cave under the snow!"

Right away Little Jim's happy face came up out of the hole he had made when he had landed in the drift. The red cap on his head was covered with snow. He looked as if he had fallen into a flour barrel.

I must confess I had cringed all over when he disappeared like that, remembering Marthy's experience. I was afraid he had broken through into a bear's den and landed right on one. "Look out down there!" I yelled to him. "You might be in a bear's winter sleeping place! There might be a bear down there!"

Right that second he began to struggle to regain his balance, slipped, and slid farther down into the hole and under the tree trunk. I didn't have time to wonder if there *was* a bear there, or if it had grabbed him by the feet and pulled him under, because he yelled a muffled yell back to us saying, "Come on in! The snow's fine!"

Satisfied there wasn't any actual bear there, Poetry and I worked our way down to where Little Jim was. The place was about the size that would hold a large bear. There were leaves and marsh grass and old pine needles mashed down into a nest. But instead of their being dry as they should have been for a nice cozy bed, they were wet. On one end of the nest, water was dripping in from the melting snow overhead, and at the other end, near the trunk, the snow was broken away. It made a large exit, reminding me of a giant cocoon back at Sugar Creek with a hole in one end where the larva, after turning into a butterfly, had crawled out.

Poetry was first to say what was what, and this is what he said: *"This,* gentlemen, is where our barefoot, five-toed bear had his winter quarters!"

I'd never seen Little Jim as bright as he was that day. He was quick on the trigger with a witty remark. "Which of his quarters—his fore or his hind?"

But Poetry was right. This *had* to be the place.

"I don't blame him for getting out of bed. I'd do the very same thing myself if water started dripping down in my face and all over me," I said.

We must have been making quite a lot of noise, hollering and talking loudly, for soon there were yelling voices from the direction of the lodge. There came Big Jim, Circus, and Dragonfly, plowing through the snow toward us to see what we'd found.

Would we *ever* have news for Barry and the old-timer!

There wasn't room enough for all of us in the hole under the tree trunk. Besides, because of the wet leaves and the two holes—one at each end now that Little Jim had accidentally made the second one—it wasn't a good place to make a hideout for ourselves.

We all waded around in the snow at the place where the bear had come out. Sure enough, there were tracks like those we'd seen at the cache—large tracks with five toes, looking very much like those of a large barefoot man, except that the big toe was in the middle and there were two little toes on each foot. Also we saw the tracks of the front feet, like a large five-toed dog's or wolf's, with the claw marks quite plain.

"How big do you suppose he is?" Dragonfly asked, his teeth chattering.

"Terribly big!" Poetry said, growling the words.

On our way back to the lodge I was feeling a little worried, so I couldn't enjoy the "let's pretend" game the gang was playing as we shuffled along through the drifts, different ones taking the part of the different bears in the story "Goldilocks and the Three Bears."

Little Jim's mouselike voice did sound cute as he took the part of the baby bear, saying, "Some boy has been breaking through the roof of my house and scattering snow all over my bed!"

We'd forgotten to look for the kingfisher's home in the low bank up the lake. We'd found something else much more exciting.

We talked about different things while we cleaned our six perch at the sink. Getting our water out of the iron pump inside the house, the water pouring from its spout right into the sink, certainly was handy. I'd have to tell Dad about that when I got home. It'd save Theodore Collins's son a lot of steps to have a pump *inside* the house—and in the wintertime it wouldn't freeze up and have to be thawed out every morning before we could have fresh water.

As he had done every time we cleaned a mess of fish, the Everards' tomcat came to excited life, but he didn't get by with stealing a fish this time. We made him eat fish *heads* instead of whole fish, and he wasn't allowed to get up onto the worktable.

Noon came, and Barry and old Ed hadn't come back yet, so we ate our fish and some pancakes Poetry made for us, using a mix that told on the package how to make them.

We kept the fire going in the fireplace, even though we hardly needed it because the weather was so warm. Then we lazed around after doing the dishes, some of us taking naps because of the fire's making us drowsy. Others of us leafed through magazines, and I read a little in one of Barry's books. Two books especially interested my mind, one of them on skiing and the other on winter wildlife.

I moseyed through page after page until all of a sudden I came to with a start at something I heard on the roof of the house. *"Hey!"* I exclaimed, all the sleepiness out of me.

Little Jim, who was leaning against the wall

by the window, jumped as if he had been shot at. Dragonfly, on a chair at the table with his head buried against his arm, came to with a jerk that threw him off balance. He landed on the floor on top of Poetry's stomach—Poetry had been lying there asleep. Circus called out from the couch he was lying on, "Keep still, so I can sleep!" and turned his face to the wall.

Only Big Jim didn't react. He kept his nose buried in the book he'd been reading, which I'd seen was named *Etiquette for Boys*. The book, I'd noticed, was open to a chapter called "Your First Date."

I might have known Big Jim was old enough to be interested in a book like that. It wasn't going to be easy for the gang when he got old enough to think girls were people and wanted to be extrakind to some special girl and then maybe wouldn't have as much time to be with the gang. In fact, ever since the new minister had come to our church at Sugar Creek, he had been combing his hair better on account of the minister's daughter Sylvia. She was about his age and was very nice for a girl. She was polite and pretty, and her once-in-a-while smile at Big Jim was like her name sounded, kind of silvery.

Anyway, when I heard something on the lodge roof and yelled out, *"Hey!"* Big Jim was the only one who didn't show any reaction. He just kept on reading with his eyes glued to the chapter on "Your First Date."

Pretty soon he had to react, though, for I

was out of my easy chair and racing to the heavy oak door to unbolt it and yank it open to see what was going on.

6

Before I could get to the door, there was a rumbling noise on the roof as if an animal—or a ghost—was using it for a slide. As fast as greased lightning, whatever was up there slid off and landed somewhere just outside the door with a *clatterety-thuddety-scrish!*

What I expected to see when I did open the door, I didn't know, but probably some kind of wildlife—a porcupine, maybe—that had been climbing one of the twin pines and had accidentally lost his hold on a branch, fallen onto the roof, and rolled all the way down.

"Oh, no!" I exclaimed in disappointment when I saw nothing but a pile of wet snow on the porch, so close to the door we'd have to scoop it aside to get out.

"Snow's melting off the roof," I started to say. I also started to look up.

I stopped talking and looking when there was another rumbling above my head. Before I could get my head out of the way, an avalanche of watery snow whammed down on me, making me yell so loud I could have been heard as far away as the kingfisher's hole in the bluff up the lake.

It was like the noise of Santa and his reindeer on the lawn in the poem most people know. On our lodge porch there arose such a clatter that Circus and Poetry and Dragonfly and Little Jim sprang from their sleep to see what was the matter.

What had happened wasn't important, except that it shows how warm the weather really was. And warm weather meant that things in the north woods were anything but normal. Unless there was a cold spell soon, there wouldn't be any frozen North.

It was this same warm weather that had melted the snow and made the bear's sleeping quarters so uncomfortable that he had to get out and hunt up a new place.

Weather could certainly make a boy's vacation interesting, and a change in the weather could make a change in his vacation activities.

Well, the avalanche from the roof did wake us all up and sent us outdoors to make snowballs. The new snow was just right.

"Let's make a statue of Old Timber," Little Jim suggested.

We voted that down because we knew we could never make a wolf's four slender legs strong enough to hold up his body. We decided on a bear. We patterned it after one we had seen a picture of in one of Barry's books. We certainly had a lot of fun doing it, expecting any minute to see Barry and the old-timer come driving up the lane in Ed's Jeep pickup.

Little Jim's eyes always had a faraway look in them when he was pretending anything, and he kept coming up with bright ideas. "We're making a wife for the bear that's been sleeping under the fallen tree," he said, as he grunted along, pushing the snowball he'd been rolling for quite a while.

We were very careful not to obliterate the tracks of the *real* bear that had been walking around on his hind feet under the cache. These we wanted Barry and Mr. Wimbish to see, as well as the abandoned den under the fallen tree.

Another thing Little Jim's very bright, alert little mind thought to say was: "The father bear's name is Adam. He lives all alone in the Garden of Eden, and he doesn't have any wife, so we're making one for him."

Dragonfly knew the Bible story, too, but he was skeptical of Little Jim's idea. "God used a rib out of the man to make his wife. We're making the *bear's* wife out of snow! Besides, the man Adam was asleep when God took the rib out of his side. Our bear is wide awake and maybe a mile or two or three away from here."

We were nearly finished when Little Jim came up with another bright idea. "We've got Father Bear and Mother Bear. Now let's make a *baby* bear."

When, quite a while later, we had finished, our work really looked good. It was easy to stand back about forty feet and imagine our Mother Bear was brownish-black or coal black in color with a tiny white spot on her breast as bears sometimes have, her face having a little cinnamon-brown color, her hair long and not quite soft, not quite hard, her tail not much longer than a cottontail's, her claws long and sharp and curved a little. And her fierce teeth ready to eat up anybody who interrupted her in something she was already eating.

The baby bear we made was as cute as a bug's ear and looked more like a bear than his mother did. We were quite proud of ourselves and kept wishing Barry and Mr. Wimbish would hurry up.

"He's as pretty as a picture," Little Jim exclaimed, pride on his small face because he was the one who had thought of making the baby bear in the first place. He started to stroke the snowy top of the baby bear's skull.

It was the word "picture" that gave Poetry an idea. "Let's make a *real* bear!" he all of a sudden cried excitedly, with so much enthusiasm in his voice that it shot a thrill through me.

"I need two strong men," he ordered. "Come on! Hurry, while the sun is still out."

The second he said it, the sun went under a cloud.

A few minutes later I knew what his idea was. The two strong men he had asked for—Big Jim and Circus—came out of the lodge carrying the big bearskin rug, the one that had been made out of the bear the old-timer had stabbed and Marthy had shot dead with her .300 Magnum rifle.

Next, we found a man's raincoat in the lodge closet, which maybe belonged to Mr. Everard, and spread it over the mother bear's snow statue, so that the inside of the bearskin rug wouldn't get wet. Then we all worked together, grunting and grinning and growling like real bears until we had the rug spread out and tucked around the snow bear in such a way as to make it look like an honest-to-goodness live black bear. We had to use extra snow, packing it all around, so it'd look as if our bear was stomach-deep in a drift.

Standing back and studying it while Poetry stood waiting for a few seconds of sunlight so he could get a good picture, I was feeling fine that the bearskin rug, having under it a form that was shaped like a live bear, looked pretty savage. Its powerful incisors looked very dangerous. So also did the rest of its teeth. Its mouth was open and its nose wrinkled into a snarl.

Poetry was just about to snap the picture when Little Jim yelled, "Wait! Let me be socking her on the head with a club."

It was a good idea. Pretty soon Little Jim was standing beside the bear, holding a club in his hands, upraised as if he was about to wham an honest-to-goodness wild bear on her fierce nose.

Different ones of us got our pictures taken with the bear. Dragonfly wanted to be sitting on it, as though he was on a horse; Circus stood on it. Big Jim worked his arm into the jaws and made a terrible grimace as if he was suffering what he called "excruciating pain."

It was good fun, and we would have some excitement at home when we showed the pictures to our friends and especially to our parents.

The sun was still high, even though it kept going under some fast-moving clouds. We'd still have time to go out to the shanty and back. We'd probably get some whoppers this time and have them sizzling in the pan for Barry and Ed Wimbish when they came into camp from their trapline trip.

"We'll leave the rug on her," Big Jim said. "That bear's so real-looking, they'll think it's an honest-to-goodness live one. It'll be a good joke to play on them."

"Better leave a note telling them where we went, just in case they get back before we do," Poetry thought to say, and Big Jim ordered him to do it.

"I'll help you," I said to Poetry, and away the two of us went.

Being good on a typewriter, Poetry plunked himself down on the chair at the table and, using Barry's machine, quick had the note ready. When it was finished, he handed it to me with a grin, saying, "That'll let him know we think it's all right for him to stop being our camp director next June."

"But we're not glad about it," I answered.

We left the typed note lying in the center of the dining table, putting a paperweight on it so that, in case it was windy when he and old Ed came in, the note wouldn't blow off onto the floor or into the fireplace.

"It's a good thing we came back," Poetry

exclaimed. "I almost forgot my camera. I want a picture of myself hauling in a nine-pound walleye."

The gang was waiting for us at the kingfisher's tree. For a minute I stood looking up at the place where ordinarily the ridiculous-looking bird was perched, but his branch was empty. Only for a second, though. All of a sudden, there was a whirring and a shadow of wings in the sky, and there our new friend was. The branch he had landed on was shaking as hard as a branch that size does back at Sugar Creek when a blue jay comes shooting across the sky to suddenly drop down on it feetfirst.

"Hey, you up there!" I exclaimed to my rattling-voiced friend. "Don't get in such a hurry for supper! You just had *dinner!*"

"That was *lunch,*" Dragonfly said. "He wants his *dinner* now."

I gave Dragonfly a "let's pretend" angry scowl and answered, "Kingfishers up here are the same as they are at Sugar Creek. They have breakfast, dinner, and supper."

At the clump of evergreens, near the beginning of the "road" out to the shanty and just before we started the long trek across the frozen, snow-covered lake, Dragonfly, who was quite a ways ahead of the rest of us, yelled back, "Hey, you guys! Come here quick! Here's the bear's tracks again!"

The minute he said that, going fishing in an ice shanty seemed like nothing. The great big wish I'd had to trail the bear to see where he had holed up again, if he had—or maybe to see the actual bear—blew itself up in my mind like a balloon. I wanted desperately to follow the bear!

I tried to keep my voice indifferent as I suggested to Big Jim, "If we knew which way he went, we could tell Barry and Mr. Wimbish, so they could find his trail easier when they get back."

"We're going to stay in sight of the camp," Big Jim answered, and I noticed that his fuzz-covered upper lip was set, meaning I'd better not suggest again that we follow the bear.

Dragonfly was already hurrying along on the bear's trail. "He's following the shoreline!" he cried excitedly.

I looked back toward the lodge, and the big birchwood letters spelling out Snow Goose were as plain as day.

A bright idea popped into my mind then and, just as quick, flew on word wings straight toward Dragonfly about a hundred feet ahead of us. "We have to stay in sight of the lodge! The very second his tracks lead off into the forest out of sight of the lodge, we have to stop trailing him!"

"You little rascal of a schemer!" Big Jim said to me and slapped me a friendly slap on the shoulder. "But you've solved my problem. I wanted to follow his tracks myself but didn't dare because of my promise to Barry to stay within sight of the lodge. We'll go as far as we can."

"I've got my compass," Poetry said cheerfully, "just in case we happen to have to go a little way back into the brush."

"We're *not* going to run any risks," Big Jim replied firmly.

And so we started out, not interested in ice fishing anymore—not with a bigger fish in a fur coat roaming the woods.

Poetry kept his camera in readiness, waiting for a chance to take a picture of any kind of wildlife we happened onto, to help Barry with his important paper. He got several shots of different things. One shot was of the Snow Goose, to prove to Barry that while we were trailing the bear, we could actually see the lodge, even though it was quite a distance away. He had to take a few of his pictures without any sunlight, though.

Because the trail kept following the shoreline of the bay, it was easy to stay in sight of camp except when our backs were turned to it.

You'd have thought that bear was drunk, the way he had kept going this way and that, over and around fallen logs, and retracing his steps after going up to a high brush pile or fallen tree.

Little Jim seemed to be enjoying himself almost more than anybody else. He swung along through the snow, grunting and grinning and swinging his stick as he always did back home. Once he came out with a very bright idea when he said, "The poor mother bear back there by the cache, with her cute little baby bear, is lonesome for the father bear, and we're out hunting for him to bring him home to his family."

Would we actually find the father bear? I wondered. It seemed maybe we might, although his trail kept winding round and round, and it took a lot of time to get anywhere.

The tracks were still as if the bear was drunk, and he certainly didn't act as if he had been in any hurry.

"I'll bet he's so sleepy he can't see straight," Dragonfly suggested.

I knew what he meant. I'd been that way myself sometimes, after going to sleep on the sofa of our living room when I should have gone to bed first. I could hardly get up the stairs, fumble my way out of my clothes, and fall into bed.

Circus, who was ahead of the rest of us most of the time, found two or three places that looked suspicious. When he first saw them, he thought he'd found the bear's new hibernating place. But always the tracks went on—and on and on and on.

"Hey, you guys!" Dragonfly yelled once. "Here's a big cave back in the cliff! I'll bet he's in there!"

Poetry had his camera ready for a snapshot, but when we got to where Dragonfly was, Poetry let out an explosive breath, saying, "Goose! Didn't you see his tracks going in and coming out again? There they go! Around that old Norway pine tree!"

Poetry was right.

After maybe a half hour of winding round and round, always getting a little farther around the bay and also farther from the Snow Goose, and after we'd found three more places where the bear had decided not to spend the rest of his winter, Big Jim said, "He must be a snooty old quadruped. Can't say I blame him, though. Not after what happened to his last bed."

The tracks kept *on* going, always staying not more than a hundred yards from shore, and only a few times did we have to go deep enough into the forest so that we couldn't strain our eyes through the trees toward the Snow Goose and actually see it. Every time we did, Big Jim halted us and sent Circus on ahead to look, while he and the rest of us stayed behind where the lodge was visible.

"Bear or no bear," Big Jim barked to us again and again, "orders are orders! If we don't obey Barry, he'll never trust us alone again."

And then, all of a sudden, Circus, up ahead of us, stopped stock-still and stood tense. He quick turned and motioned with his hands and face for us to come quick, his expression showing that at last he had found what we were looking for.

It didn't take us long to get to where Circus was, and we crept up as quietly as we could.

"*Sh!*" he shushed us, with his finger to his lips.

I could see the tracks zigzagging through the shrubbery in the direction of a fallen tree like the one under which we'd found his other hibernating place.

I could feel my heart pounding in my temples. *This,* I thought, *is a brand-new experience for you. This is what you wanted.*

We gathered in a football huddle, wondering what to do. You just didn't walk up to a bear's bedroom without letting him know you were coming—*if* you were coming.

"I want a picture of the entrance," Poetry said, getting his camera ready.

"We'll circle the place first, to see if there are any tracks leading away," Big Jim said.

In a few minutes we were making a wide circle, staying within about fifty feet of the base of the tree, where the snow was piled high, blown there by the winter winds.

"Look!" Dragonfly whispered to whoever was close enough to hear him. He was peering through the dead leaves of a thicket of dwarf oak. The leaves were still hanging on the way oak leaves do nearly all winter. "See? There's the big hole where he went in!"

There was a big hole, all right. The only thing was that the den—or nest—wasn't very deep. Only a few feet back inside, you could see as plain as day that it was filled with pine branches and snow and other stuff, as though whatever had gone in had tried to block the entrance.

"That's to keep Old Timber from coming in to wake him up, I'll bet," Little Jim piped.

But his idea got squelched when Poetry said,

"That's to keep out the winter winds. *Br-r-r-r!* Say, you guys! Do you realize it's beginning to get cold?"

I'd noticed it myself but had been so intent on trailing the bear I'd paid little attention. I'd zipped up my winter jacket, though, and had been keeping my hands in my pockets for the past half hour or so, since I'd not worn any mittens.

"Let's see if there *are* any tracks leading away," Circus said.

And right away we finished making our complete circle, all the way back to the long fallen pine and around it to where we had been in the first place. That is, we went *almost* all the way around, for there, at the base of the fallen tree, we saw something that made us all let out a groan at the same time. Right in front of our eyes was another large hole in the snowdrift, and tracks leading away, this time out into the forest.

It was disgustingly disappointing. "That father bear certainly is particular what kind of bed he sleeps in!" Little Jim said.

Looking back, I could see, away out in the middle of the lake, the row of evergreens that was the road leading back to the Snow Goose. I couldn't *see* the lodge from where we were, but I *could* see the shore, and from there I knew the lodge was just across the bay a half mile or so.

First making absolutely sure the bear wasn't in the hollow under the tree, we went in and looked around.

Big Jim let out a whistle and exclaimed. "Feel here with your bare hands, will you? The ground is warm yet! He's been gone maybe only a few minutes!"

My fears came to life for a second, long enough for me to say, "The three bears in the story of Goldilocks came back while she was still in their house. We'd better get out of here!"

Out of there I got but was immediately hit in the face by swirling snow from the top of the drift. The wind certainly had gotten stronger the past fifteen minutes. That bear had better decide on a place to spend the winter pretty soon, or he'd find himself really needing his fur coat, I thought.

"Maybe he stayed out long enough to begin to get hungry. Maybe the warmer weather fooled him into thinking it was spring and time to get out of bed. Look here," Big Jim said. "He's been digging into this old decayed stump for grubs or something!"

"I'll bet he wasn't even looking for a place to sleep," Circus suggested. "He was doing what hungry bears do—looking for the larva of june bugs and plant roots."

"OK, you guys," Poetry ordered us. "Stay here a minute. I'll get out and take a picture of all of you coming out of hibernation!"

He looked out and all around to see where the sun was, so that he could get it behind his back for the best picture.

"Sun's gone into hibernation, too, looks like," he said.

I followed the circle his eyes had taken and saw in the sky only a lot of fast-moving clouds that acted as if they were in a hurry to get from one side of the sky to the other.

By the time Poetry had us placed where he wanted us, our heads in a huddle looking out of the den, and had snapped our picture a few times—then had me snap his with his head where mine had been—quite a lot of time had passed.

The bear's tracks were leading deeper into the forest, so we knew we couldn't follow them any farther.

And then, all of a sudden, we heard a strange yet somehow familiar sound, one we'd heard before back home when one of the worst blizzards in Sugar Creek history came roaring in and caught us out in the middle of the woods in Old Man Paddler's hills.

What a blizzard *that* was! And what a time we had had getting to shelter! The nearest place of shelter was a haunted house. No wonder we decided to name that story *Lost in the Blizzard*.

"Listen!" Big Jim yelled, so he could be sure we'd hear him.

I'd already heard it—a sound like the droning of a million bees in the trees overhead and all around us.

I looked all around and up and saw clouds of blowing snow driving through the trees and shrubbery between us and the lake. The air over the lake itself was alive with a swirling, blinding wall of white. The "road" evergreens, scarcely visible, were tossing wildly in the wind. The storm had come up as fast as a Sugar Creek summer storm, which sometimes roars in out of the northwest, knocking over trees and small outbuildings, making tumbleweeds out of our chicken coops, and rolling our rain barrel across the yard before whamming it against the fence as if it was light as a feather.

I might have guessed the nervous clouds that had started racing across the sky in the middle of the afternoon meant a storm was coming, especially when all of a sudden, a half hour ago, the wind changed directions and had been blowing steadily harder ever since.

"Everybody stay together!" Big Jim ordered. "And follow me to the lake! We'll be all right if we follow the shoreline! We can't miss the lodge!"

"That's almost two miles to go home following the shore!" Circus protested. "If we could get out to the row of evergreens, we could be there in half the time."

Just then a fierce gust of wind blew my cap off, and I saw it go sailing like a kite with the string broken back toward the fallen tree we'd just left. The wind mussed up my hair, and snow blew down my neck. Boy oh boy! It *was* cold! "My *hat!*" I cried. "I gotta go back and get it!"

Circus, being a faster runner than the rest of us, and maybe stronger, plowed ahead of me and got to the hat first.

"Thanks a million," I gasped—and I mean *really* gasped, because the wind caught my words and tossed them away into the woods as though I hadn't even said them.

"Father Bear had better be getting home!" he puffed to me as we plowed our way back to where the gang was—Big Jim had made them stay with him so not a one of us would be lost.

The closer we got to the lake, the harder the wind blew—and the colder. It seemed the late afternoon had suddenly turned to late twilight. In fact, the snow was coming down so hard that it was like white night all around us.

It was just as if the blizzard had been waiting for us to get to the lake, where it had planned to meet us, for the minute we got there, the storm struck. It came screaming in like a wild thing, tearing through the leafless trees and evergreens, driving snow ahead of it, completely hiding the sky, the trees we had left behind, and those that had been visible bordering the shore itself.

Little Jim expressed it for all of us when his small voice yelled, "It's like a great big giant as big as Paul Bunyan with a scoop as wide as the sky scattering whole forestfuls of snow all over everything!"

It also sounded as if the giant was panting hard, his breath coming out eighty miles an hour.

Looking ahead of us out onto the lake where our road was supposed to be was like looking into a white tornado. We couldn't any more see the road than anything.

"We shoulda crawled into the bear's den ourselves!" Poetry yelled. "We'd have been sheltered there!"

"We'd have *frozen!*" Big Jim shouted back, struggling along ahead of the rest of us. "It'll be twenty below zero before morning! You know how it does back home!"

At the lakeshore, we dropped down behind a fallen log, against which brush had been piled by someone cutting wood. Sheltered for a minute against the driving wind, we could hear each other talk.

"We've got to decide something quick," Big Jim said.

"Decide what?" Dragonfly asked, and his worried voice showed he was beginning to be afraid.

Big Jim's answer was hardly audible as the wind whipped in over the top of our shelter and caught his words away, but I heard them anyway and they were:

"We've got to decide whether to take the long way around, following the shore, and run the risk of getting bogged down in drifts—maybe not getting to the lodge for two hours—or make a beeline out into the lake to the evergreens and follow them straight across to the Snow Goose! *We've got to get back before it's too dark!*"

7

We decided on the beeline from the shore to the evergreen road.

Big Jim certainly knew how to give orders, and because a lot was at stake—six lives, maybe —we obeyed. "I'll fight on ahead, breaking a path," he said, "and the rest of you follow in this order: Little Jim, Dragonfly, Bill, Poetry, and Circus. And, listen, every one of you— don't a one of you dare leave the path I'm breaking! We've got to stay together!"

Stay together we did. Every few seconds Big Jim called the roll, and we answered him as we did at the one-room red brick school back at Sugar Creek—although we wouldn't dare *yell*, "Here!" in school the way we did when Big Jim called out our names.

I had never been in such a wild wind, and I hope I'll never have to spend a worried half hour like that again as long as I live. The wind wasn't as cold yet as I knew it was bound to get before morning, but it was driving against us, cutting into my bare face and pounding down inside my collar.

Little Dragonfly, being short of breath most of the time anyway, had it pretty rough, but I stayed right behind him, shoving him along and helping him when he was staggering around for balance.

All I could see, past the heads of Dragonfly and Little Jim, was the strong, broad back of Big Jim, head down, pushing into the storm, breaking snow and also breaking the driving wind for the smaller guys who struggled behind him. There wasn't a sign of any of the evergreens yet—not even one of them. We'd been battling the storm for what seemed a terribly long time before we woke up to the fact that we should have found the "road" quite a while ago.

"You got your compass?" Big Jim shouted back at Poetry.

We gathered into a huddle around Poetry's compass, but it was too dark to see its face.

Lucky for us, though, his compass was part of a combination matchbox *and* compass. We struck a match, shielding its flame the best we could with our bodies, and the match stayed lit just long enough to see which direction was north.

I was remembering Mom's advice on the telephone while we'd been back in the hotel, and it felt good that we really had a compass to tell directions. For just one second, I wondered if my parents were worrying about me. They certainly would if they knew where I was—or wasn't. I wasn't sure where I was or wasn't, myself.

"North is *this* way, right behind me," Poetry puffed. "This is the way to go."

"You gotta go *east* from the lakeshore," Dragonfly put in.

"*East?*" Big Jim exclaimed. "We just *came* from the east."

After maybe three minutes of cold worry, we all came to realize that it didn't help us a tiny bit to know where north was, because we didn't know where *we* were. We might have already passed the row of trees, maybe gone between two of them without seeing either one. We could be away out in the middle of the lake by now.

It wasn't exactly the happiest time I'd ever had in my life. You get a terribly lost feeling when you're lost and know it.

We'd had all kinds of advice on what to do when you're lost, but not a one of the rules told us what to do if you're lost in the middle of a snowstorm and can't see anything in any direction except blinding snow.

And I never knew it to get dark so fast.

Dragonfly's suggestion was as crazy as any I'd ever heard when he said, "One of the rules for finding your way when you're lost is to climb a tree and look around."

"Out here on the lake," Big Jim remarked grimly, "trees don't grow on bushes."

We changed our plans at Big Jim's orders. We held hands, stretched ourselves out in as long a line as we could, and started to struggle along again, hoping to find the row of evergreens.

We kept the littlest kids in the middle, with Circus and Big Jim on the ends. Our line wasn't more than fifteen feet from end to end, but we hadn't gasped our way along for more than five minutes before somebody let out a yell, crying, "Here's a tree! Here's the road! We're saved!"

Now we could get home easily. All we had to do was follow the line of trees till we got to the shore and then push on to the lodge. Once inside, we'd be safe, warm, and all right.

It wasn't any easy-as-pie work to follow the tree road, because the trees had been set quite a distance apart. But one after another of them came into view as we battled our way through the drifting snow.

"Can't be long now!" Poetry cried, shouting into my ear so that I could hear, because the wind was so wild and noisy against my face and ears and all of me. "Only six more trees—if we found the first one where I think we did."

After another five minutes, with the wind seeming to get colder every second and the snow cutting our faces worse, Big Jim let out a yell. "I see it! We're there!"

The sound of his shout sent a thrill of happiness through me in spite of the cold. I'd been praying for help. It seemed I'd been asking for quite a while that we'd be able to get back to the lodge safely. I'd been thinking of Little Jim and especially of Dragonfly, who was having such a hard time getting his breath and was about ready to drop.

What I'd been praying for especially was that Mom wouldn't have anything to make her sorry she'd let me go on our winter vacation.

For a second or two, when it had looked as if maybe we wouldn't get back and might all freeze to death, I'd seen with my mind's eye a little white casket in our living room. In it was a red-haired, freckle-faced boy. It also seemed I wasn't there but had already gone to heaven where Old Man Paddler's wife, Sarah, was.

But that was for only a second. I knew I hadn't actually gone to heaven because of the driving wind in my face and the stinging snow and the cold. Also I was praying and asking forgiveness for any sins I couldn't think of right then, as well as for a few I could. Then, for a fleeting second, I seemed to see through the storm a big wooden cross planted in the ground on a small hill and the Savior hanging there, dying in my place for my sins. "Thank You . . ." I started to say.

But Big Jim's shout, *"I see it! We're there!"* interrupted my thoughts and whirled them away into nothingness. I was still alive and all right, and we had reached the lodge.

But it turned out that we *weren't* there. Circus realized it first and yelled to all of us, "It's the bobhouse! *We've come the wrong direction!*"

And we had.

How on earth we'd happened to do it, I don't know—and it didn't make any difference now. At least we had shelter from the blizzard. In only a few minutes we had scooped the snow from the door, unfastened the latch, and were inside out of the biting wind.

We were also in the dark, so Poetry's matchbox came in handy. So also did the kerosene lantern on the shelf, which the very first match showed us was still there.

Big Jim gave quick attention to the stove and soon had a fire going.

It was wonderful to be inside and safe. We certainly were glad the old-timer had built the house strong and weatherproof. But it wasn't worry-proof, and we had a lot of things to be concerned about.

Poetry's note at the lodge would let Barry or Ed know where we were—that is, if they could get back without getting stuck in a drift somewhere. What if they were out in the storm themselves?

Had anybody tried to phone us to see if we were all right? And when we hadn't been there to answer the phone, were they worried half to death?

Dragonfly expressed it for us when he whined, "What if when our folks back home listen to the news on the radio and hear about the storm up here and try to phone us, and nobody answers at the lodge?"

But Little Jim knocked a hole in that worry. He just said, "If we have to stay all night, I get to sleep up there in the upper berth!"

One thing was sure: it'd be crazy to go out into that howling blizzard and try to follow our "road" across to the Snow Goose. There was a stack of dry wood in the shanty and a larger rick outside. After we brushed the snow off, it would burn all right.

"There's enough wood to keep us warm all night and all day tomorrow, if we have to stay that long," I said.

"I'm hungry," Dragonfly whined, and so were we all.

"We can have fish for supper," Big Jim answered him. "But we'll have to catch them first."

Poetry was mischievous at the wrong time and in the wrong way when he said, "I've got a plastic bag of night crawlers in my coat pocket. We could fry them—"

He didn't even get to finish his nonsensical sentence, because right that second the wind whammed at the door, and something heavy struck it full force, shaking the house and scaring us plenty.

What on earth—in a blizzard!

We waited in almost deathly silence, wondering what kind of wild animal we'd get to see, maybe, and to tell Barry about for his special paper.

When, after a few minutes, there wasn't any further sound except that of snow and howling wind, Big Jim opened the door a crack to see what was what.

He exclaimed a second later, "The wind's left us a Christmas tree!"

I'd seen it, too. Caught against the door latch was one of the trees Mr. Wimbish had set in the ice and snow to mark the evergreen road. "We couldn't get back now if we wanted to," I said. "Looks like the storm is blowing our road away."

We'd *have* to stay all night now, even if we'd been brave enough or foolhardy enough to try to follow the line of evergreens to the lodge.

But you just couldn't discourage Little Jim. He piped up with another cute idea—which was not really good—when he said cheerfully, "Don't they make these fish shanties on sled runners? So they can move them from a worn-out fishing place to a new one?"

I'd heard somewhere that they did, and said so. Then Little Jim finished the idea that had started in his mind: "The way the wind's blowing out there, maybe we'll wake up in the morning and find ourselves parked on the shore out in front of the Snow Goose!"

It was a cute idea, but Dragonfly spoiled it for him by saying, "More'n likely the wind'd blow our house *over!*"

Poetry joined in with Little Jim's cheerful mood by tossing into the conversation his own bright remark, "Then I'll huff and I'll puff and I'll blow your house in."

That was the wrong thing to say, because Dragonfly's next sad words were, "What if Old Timber gets cold out in the storm and starts looking for a nice warm place to spend the night?"

And that *was* the wrong thing to say. It started a whirlwind-sized worry spiraling in my own mind, which in only a few seconds was like a small tornado. I wasn't worried about Old Timber. Wolves didn't hibernate. But *bears* did!

Right that very minute, maybe, old Father Bear was outside somewhere, sleepy and grumpy and maybe even hungry, trying to find a warm shelter so he could go back to sleep until spring. What nicer, cozier place in the whole north woods than a fishing shanty like the one we ourselves were in!

"Wolves don't hibernate!" I said to Dragonfly, and he quick came out with the very worry that was bothering me, saying, "But *bears* do!"

Big Jim broke into the conversation then, his words hardly audible over the noise his poker was making as he stirred up the fire in the stove. His face looked a little worried in the yellow light of the flames. "Our bear's probably gone back to the last place he left—or maybe all the way back to where he spent the first half of his winter. The last tracks I saw were headed back."

"It's the baby bear I'm worried about," Little Jim piped up. "He hasn't any fur coat like his father and mother have."

Circus yawned as though he was sleepy and grunted. "The way the wind's blowing, Mother Bear's fur coat'll probably be blown off and we'll find it somewhere out in the woods when we get back tomorrow."

"If there is any tomorrow." That was Dragonfly's sad answer.

I was surprised to hear Big Jim's half-angry order right then, as he demanded of all of us,

"Let's can the discouraging talk! We're safe and warm, and we ought to show a little trust."

I knew what he meant when he said "trust." Big Jim was one of the finest Christian boys I'd ever met. He had been even better since Sylvia had moved to Sugar Creek. When he said "trust," I knew he meant faith in God. We ought to show a little faith that the heavenly Father was looking after us. Hadn't He led us through a blinding blizzard all the way to the shanty? Hadn't He helped us find the row of evergreens before the wind started blowing them away?

Pretty soon we had our trapdoors open and were catching fish. When we'd caught enough, we quick cleaned them and after tossing the heads and entrails outside, we started up the camp stove. Using the salt and pepper and lard that were there, we had a fish supper.

A little later we wrapped ourselves in the blankets from the high shelf and went to bed as best we could. The small house was not made for that many boys to sleep in, but we used the benches and the upper berth and also the tabletop.

Big Jim decided we'd better save kerosene by blowing out the lantern. With a huff and a puff he did it, and the only light left was that of the flames showing through the cracks in the stove.

How long I'd slept, I didn't know. I'd had quite a time keeping warm, in spite of the fire, the blanket I had over me, and all my clothes.

It seemed I'd *almost* waked up quite a few times because of being cold. But I'd had gone back to sleep in spite of the wind that shook our house and made me think of Little Jim's idea that we might wake up in the morning on the shore near the lodge.

And then all of a sudden I *was* wide awake, sitting up on my bench bunk, my heart pounding, my worried eyes looking about at the strange shadows of things—the other boys asleep all around me, the stack of wood not far from the stove, the sturdy picnic table with Circus and Big Jim sleeping on it.

The flickering light from the stove made everything look ghostlike, especially to a scared-half-to-death boy, which it seemed right that second I was. I didn't know why. Something had jerked me to a sitting position with all the sleep knocked out of me.

The face of Poetry, who'd been sleeping nearest me, was like that of a frightened, mussed-up-haired ghost. His husky whisper came across the few feet of space between us: *"Did you hear that?"*

Had I *heard* it! I most certainly had. Just one second before he asked his question, there'd been what sounded like a scream outside, not far from the shanty door.

Before I could answer Poetry, there was another high-pitched cry that sent a shower of shivers all over me. I knew the door Ed had built was strong, but any large wild animal that wanted to could break it down.

The weird, wailing sound that had shattered my sleep all to smithereens was enough to give even the most experienced woodsman the heebie-jeebies.

The rest of the gang's sleep was shattered, too. "M—maybe it's the b–b–bear!" Dragonfly stammered.

"Bears don't scream," Big Jim's husky voice corrected him. Then he added in a tone that didn't agree with his words, "It might just be the house cat looking for us and smelling our fish."

But I knew his mind's eye wasn't seeing the big beautiful tomcat that had been hanging around the lodge ever since we'd been there.

I wished that was all it was, but I knew whatever I'd heard wasn't any tame animal.

"Listen," Big Jim's half-calm voice exclaimed.

There was something different about the sound this time. It wasn't a trembling caterwaul as it had seemed before. It was like a human being's voice, a frightened, exhausted cry for help.

Woman! I thought. That was what the smothered cry coming to us from somewhere out in that howling blizzard sounded like—a *woman's* high-pitched, trembling scream, calling, *"He–e–e–elp! He–e–e–elp!"*

"What'll we do?" Dragonfly's worried voice broke into my thoughts.

"Go back to sleep," Poetry suggested and yawned as if he was indifferent, the very opposite of what I knew he was. "It's probably just a wildcat. They often scream like that when they're hunting."

Before Dragonfly or anybody could disagree with him, Poetry hurried on to explain, "When a wildcat's hunting and screams like that, if there happens to be a live lunch hiding anywhere near, the scream'll scare the living daylights out of the lunch. The lunch'll jump or make some kind of animal noise. The wildcat'll hear it, and if the live lunch is the kind of animal wildcats like, in only a few minutes the wildcat won't be hungry anymore."

"That doesn't make sense!" Dragonfly showed good sense by saying. "No wildcat could hear anything jump in a blizzard. I tell you that's s–s–something else! It s–s–sounds like a w–woman!"

"He's right!" Big Jim exclaimed from where he was, near the stove, getting ready to open the firebox door and put in another chunk of fuel. He quick changed his mind about putting in more wood, and he lit the lantern instead.

I was off my bunk in a flash. If *Big Jim* thought there was a woman out there, then maybe there was.

When the lantern was lit and in place, Big Jim unbolted the door and yanked it open. The wind whipped in a flurry of snow and icy wind, almost blowing out the light.

Then, what to my wondering eyes should appear but a medium-tall, extrapretty, rosy-cheeked girl in a snow-covered dark green coat with wide fur sleeves and fur collar. She was wearing brown ski pants. On her feet, instead of boots, was a pair of snowshoes.

The second I saw her, I knew who she was.

So also did Poetry, who whispered to me, "Barry's twenty-year-old mother!" It was certainly not the right time to be thinking a mischievous thought.

She didn't breeze in happily, the way I'd seen her do back in the hotel lobby when Poetry and I had been under the potted palm. She fell in, instead, stumbling over the high sill and landing on the board floor of the shanty, striking her head against the table.

Before we could get her far enough in to close the door, I saw, not more than fifteen feet from the shanty, a pair of fiery eyes. But it was only for a fleeting flash. Then a blur of grayish snow-covered fur faded away like a ghost into the swirling snow.

"The ghost wolf!" Poetry cried. "I saw him out there!"

Two things had to be done quickly—help the girl all the way inside and get the door shut to keep out the fierce winter weather that was driving and blowing and howling like a wild animal as big as the whole north woods wilderness.

I'd never seen a young lady so exhausted. She gasped to us, "Thank God, I made it! I was afraid I wouldn't. *Aunt Martha!* I think she's having a heart attack!"

Big Jim unfastened the heel straps of the girl's snowshoes and slipped her feet out of them. In the light of the lantern on the shelf, her eyes looked terrified. She struggled to a sitting position, leaning against the table leg, and still breathing hard.

"Barry?" she cried out all of a sudden. "I thought—"

"Barry," Big Jim answered politely and in as calm a voice as he could, "went with Ed Wimbish on his trapline this morning. They haven't come back yet."

Things were pretty mixed up in my mind, and it seemed also in the mind of the girl. But as we all talked and listened, and while the wind howled outside and drove the snow against our windows, while six scared boys and one even more-worried girl tried to explain to each other why we were there at such an unearthly time, things began to untangle themselves.

This is the story as best I can give it to you:

She had driven all the way from Minneapolis to bring the station wagon here, so that we could have it to drive home in. She would spend the weekend with her Aunt Martha and Uncle Ed, but she got to the Wimbish Grocery *after* the storm had struck. The store was closed, so she drove down to the Wimbish lakeshore cottage. Martha was trying to put in a telephone call to the lodge to see if we were all right, when suddenly all the lights went out in the cottage and the phone went dead.

Martha was terribly worried because the phone had been ringing and ringing and no one had answered at the Snow Goose. She just *knew* something terrible had happened to us. The only thing to do was to try to make it out to the lodge in the station wagon.

They'd tried. They'd gotten all the way to the lane that leads in and had gotten stuck there. In desperation they'd started out on foot to the lodge. The storm seemed wilder than any they'd ever been in before.

Martha's heart seemed to be acting up when they reached there, and then she had fainted.

"I found your note on the table, but I thought Barry had left it for me, just in case I came early. I couldn't revive Martha, and the phone wasn't working, so I couldn't call anyone. It—it seemed there was only one thing to do—follow the evergreen road I knew ran out here to the shanty . . ."

She stopped explaining and raised her hand to her forehead, her eyes closed as if she was in pain.

Then I saw it for the first time—a line of red on her temple, running up into the hairline.

She slumped against the corner of the bench and went over in a crumpled heap onto the floor.

"She's f–fainted!" Little Jim cried.

And she had.

8

What do you do when you are in a fishing shanty more than a mile from camp, shut in by a blinding blizzard that seems to be getting worse every minute, and the road markers back to the lodge have maybe been blown away?

And *what* do you do when your camp director's very special friend, whom he is going to marry next June, is lying in a faint on the floor of the shanty with a trickle of blood coming from under her pretty brown hair down onto her forehead?

We not only had to give her first aid, but we had to do something about Martha Wimbish, who was back at the lodge, maybe having a heart attack—that being the reason that Barry's fiancée had fought her way through the storm to the shanty in the first place. She'd thought Barry was there, which you know he wasn't.

"My note!" Poetry whispered to me in the middle of the excitement. "It's my fault. I shouldn't have written what I did."

My mind took a run and a jump and landed in the main room of the Snow Goose, taking me along with it. It was afternoon, and I was standing behind Poetry while he typed the note to be left for Barry. It had been fun at the time, playing a joke on Barry like that. In fact, we'd set *two* joke traps for him that afternoon. The note had said, just as if Jeanne herself had typed it, "I've gone out with the boys to the shanty. If we're not back when you get here, you'll know we are having fun and catching lots of fish."

But it was the ending of the note that was the trigger of the joke trap that was to catch Barry. It was, "Looking forward to next June." Poetry hadn't signed any name.

"But we caught *her* instead of *him,*" Poetry said under his breath into my ear. "*She* read it and thought it was from him!"

And she'd fought her way out here through a dangerous storm to get help for Martha.

The other joke trap, which you already know about, we'd made by dressing a snow statue with a bear rug and leaving it to make Barry think he had seen an actual live bear, which he could write about for his important paper.

I felt more than worry in my mind for the girl lying in a faint on the floor of our shanty. I felt admiration for her. I was proud of anybody who was brave enough to fight her way through a blizzard out to where she thought Barry was to get help for her aunt. That took courage. It also took a lot of what Dad would call "stamina," which means "strength to endure."

Maybe Barry hadn't picked out such a helpless, citified girl after all.

I was thankful that Big Jim had had Scout training and knew what to do to help bring anyone out of a faint. Jeanne's being already on the floor meant that her head was low, as the head is supposed to be when you are trying to revive anyone. He quick folded one of the blankets, and we helped him put it under her hips, then elevated her feet by putting a large chunk of firewood under them. He also, in a fleeting flash of flying fingers, loosened all the tight clothing from her neck. Lifting one of the trapdoors, he dipped his handkerchief in the cold lake water and began to sponge her face with it.

Circus took orders to open one of the windows a crack to let in fresh air. It was the coldest and windiest fresh air you ever felt or breathed in your life. It took only a split second for the room to get full of it.

And a second later, Big Jim's patient revived.

He quickly put a bandage from the shanty's first-aid kit on the small open wound on the girl's head. The blood stopped flowing, and the first step in what was going to happen next was over.

"Listen!" Dragonfly cried. "The storm's getting worse! That's *thunder!*"

We didn't even have to listen to hear it. There was a roaring sound, louder than any swarm of bees could have made. It was like a prop airplane out there somewhere, with a half-dozen propellers going terribly fast.

"That's lightning!" Little Jim cried.

There wasn't any question about there being a bright light outside.

Was the world getting ready to come to an

end? Had the terrible blizzard upset nature someway and—

It was a silly question to be asking myself, but I didn't know that till a few seconds later, when the loud whirring noise came with a blaze of light right up to our shanty and stopped. I heard a door slam and footsteps crunching through the snow in our direction.

Whoever was out there, whatever he had come in, didn't bother to knock. He thrust open our shanty door, letting in a lot more unwanted weather and letting himself in with it.

"Barry!" Jeanne cried. She tried to sit up but didn't get to, because of Barry's being down on his knees beside her and—what they said and did wasn't any of six boys' business.

It seemed, though, maybe it *was* Barry's own business who was going to stand beside him in a wedding gown next June.

While the shanty door was open and before we could close it, I saw what had caused the "thunder" and "lightning." It was old Ed's four-wheel-drive Jeep with a snowplow on the front end. The engine was still running, the headlamps were still on, and its powerful spotlight was shining into our open shanty door, lighting up the whole inside.

One of the first things I heard Jeanne say was, *"Martha!* How is she? Is she all right?"

It felt good to hear Barry answer, "She's fine. She was just exhausted from walking through the snow. She's *so* fine she shot another bear! There was a bear just outside the lodge when we drove up. It seemed confused and blinded by the lights, and she thought it was trying to get inside. She grabbed the shotgun from the wall and pumped five rounds into it at close range. She'll have another bearskin rug for the lodge!"

Well, *that* news made me cringe all over. The beautiful bearskin rug, which we'd spread over and tucked in around the stomach of our mother bear's snow statue, had been riddled with maybe five hundred shotgun pellets!

Our second joke trap, set for Barry, had caught Martha instead, and it had maybe ruined a beautiful bearskin rug! Both our traps had caught the wrong people.

Barry took over from there. We would spend the rest of the night back at the lodge, he told us. The four-wheel-drive Jeep hadn't had any serious trouble getting out to us by following the tree road. A few trees were missing, blown away by the wind, he told us, but he'd been able to make it.

Jeanne and Dragonfly and Little Jim sat in the seat with Barry as he drove. Big Jim, Poetry, Circus, and I wrapped ourselves in blankets in the back. "Don't sit on the game sack!" Barry called back to us as he raced the engine, getting ready to plunge into the snowy road, which the lights showed was already blown full of fresh drifts. With the snowplow on the front, though, we could make a smooth track for the heavy-cleated tires to run in.

The back of the Jeep was open, and the

wind was working hard to keep us from keeping warm.

We hadn't any sooner started to pull away
than Circus let out an excited cry. "There goes
the shanty!"

I could see it myself through the whirling
wall of white—a big, dark, rectangular blur
being lifted up and whammed over on its side,
then turned over again and again like a tum-
bleweed on the prairie!

We'd gotten out just in time. Old Ed's carpenter work had been good, but he'd made the
shanty out of wood too light to stand a storm
with wind as hard as the one we were in.

The little old Jeep plowed right on and on
and on and on. Once we came to a place where
so many trees of the road were missing that
Barry ground to a stop and asked, "You got
your compass, Poetry?"

Poetry did have, and in a half an hour more
we were at the shore. Up the incline we went,
past the little birch and the tree that had the
dead branch at the top for the kingfisher.

Here, near the lodge, the wind was less
strong, as the tall trees and the cliff behind the
lodge protected it a little. In another second
now, we'd see the mother bear Marthy had mis-
taken for a real bear and had poured five shotgun blasts into.

The Jeep came to a grinding stop not more
than fifteen feet from the place where the ladder led up to the cache. The ladder was down,

of course, which is the way we kept it when we weren't going up or down.

"Here's Martha's bear, boys!" Barry called.

The four of us in the back tumbled out into the weather and saw in the spotlight of the Jeep, where our bear statue with the bearskin rug over it had been, the huge hulk of a savage-looking bear, sprawled half on its stomach, half on its side, in the snow.

It was pretty much covered with snow. No other bear was there. And my heart sank.

The quicker we told Barry, the better. And the quicker we got a letter off to the Everards telling them what had happened, the better. We'd offer to pay for the bearskin. If we didn't have enough money among us, we'd work hard at odd jobs back home until we'd earned enough.

One thing that made my heart sink as I waded through the snow toward where the spotlight was shining—Poetry and the rest of the gang were tumbling over each other to get there, too—was that it looked like the head of the bearskin rug had been almost blown off.

Poetry got there first. "This is *terrible!*" he exclaimed. "But how was I to know the joke would backfire?"

"It didn't," Big Jim said in a minute. He had his bare hands on the bear's neck. "This bear," he said, "is still warm. Marthy *did* shoot a real bear!"

"And–and–and there's real blood on his face!" Dragonfly cried excitedly. "We've killed a bear! A *real* bear!"

And we had.

I mean Martha had.

Just that second the lodge door opened, a shaft from a powerful flashlight shot out into the night, and Marthy's motherly voice called, "Come in, all of you! Supper's ready!"

It was the most cheerful sound I'd heard in a long time.

Out of the storm we went and into the warm lodge, a happier gang than we'd been in a long time.

"Look!" Little Jim cried to me, pointing toward the fireplace.

I looked, and there was the bearskin rug spread out on the floor, just waiting for a boy my size to come and lie down on it.

A little later, while Dragonfly was chewing an extralarge mouthful of venison, he squeezed out a few mischievous words, saying, "It's the best dinner I ever ate."

"Supper!" Little Jim corrected him.

Jeanne, the girl who was going to rob us of our camp director next June, gave Little Jim what I thought was an especially friendly smile, then said to Barry, "Your boys will hardly need a chaperone when they come back next summer. They seem to know their way around. But they *will* need a cook, and I'm willing to help do it, if they'll just let me."

It was like a heavy load all of a sudden lifted from my mind.

Later, when we were in our bunks, Poetry whispered to me, "Looks like we're not going to lose a camp director but are just going to gain a good cook."

We still had two more days before our vacation was over, but nothing very important happened—nothing, that is, to compare with all the very wonderful things we'd already experienced.

There was quite a surprise for us, though, when we went to a ski tournament the afternoon after the blizzard and discovered that our next summer's cook was one of the finest ski jumpers in the country. Barry was getting a real outdoors girl.

Then came our final morning. We were all in the station wagon, driving down to the lane toward the road that would lead us finally to the highway. Just as we were about to round the bend where we'd have our last glimpse of the Snow Goose, where we'd had one of the most wonderful weeks of our lives, all of a sudden Dragonfly, who was in the backseat with me, cried excitedly, "Look, everybody! There's Old Timber! Back there just below the cache! See! His long bushy tail—it's waving good-bye to us!"

I looked, as did we all. Barry applied the brakes, and we came to a very abrupt stop.

It was only for a few seconds that I saw him, a big, long-nosed, pointy-eared, blackish-gray, doglike animal with a gray face and whitish underparts and sides. He was standing erect, and the fur on his back was bristling as if he was angry about something.

His tail seemed to wag a little, but then it stopped, and I thought I saw his savage eyes smoldering with resentment, as if his north woods wilderness playground had been interrupted for a week and we'd better not ever come back.

A second later, it was as if we hadn't seen him at all. He just faded from sight, seemingly without moving.

A great big lonely yet happy ache came into my heart, then. The world of nature was wonderful. It seemed even more wonderful that the One who had made it was a special friend to everybody who would let Him live in their hearts.

Moody Press, a ministry of the Moody Bible Institute, is designed for education, evangelization, and edification. If we may assist you in knowing more about Christ and the Christian life, please write us without obligation: Moody Press, c/o MLM, Chicago, Illinois 60610.